THE CHILDREN OF CROW COVE SERIES
BY BODIL BREDSDORFF

The Crow-Girl

Eidi

Eidi

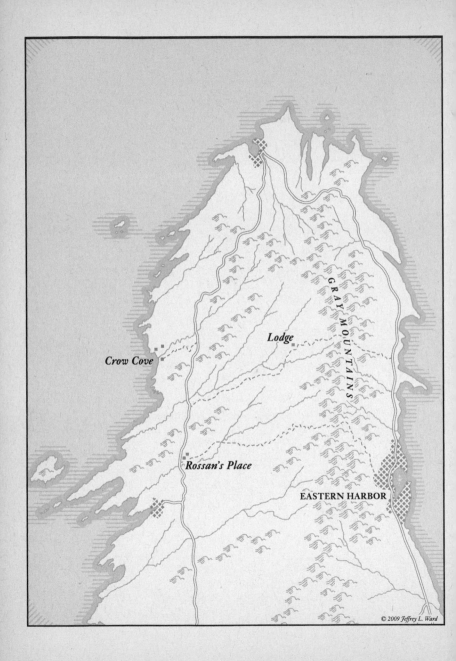

GRAY MOUNTAINS

Lodge

Crow Cove

Rossan's Place

EASTERN HARBOR

© 2009 Jeffrey L. Ward

Eidi

THE CHILDREN OF CROW COVE SERIES

BODIL BREDSDORFF

Translated from the Danish by Kathryn Mahaffy

Farrar Straus Giroux • New York

www.fsgkidsbooks.com

Library of Congress Cataloging-in-Publication Data
Bredsdorff, Bodil.
  [Eidi. English]
  Eidi / Bodil Bredsdorff ; translated from the Danish by Kathryn Mahaffy.— 1st ed.
    p. cm. — (The children of Crow Cove ; 2)
  Summary: Eidi leaves her mother and stepfather in Crow Cove to live in a
nearby village, where she meets the much younger Tink and rescues him from the
abusive man he has been living with.
  ISBN-13: 978-0-374-31267-1
  [1. Orphans—Fiction. 2. Conduct of life—Fiction.] I. Mahaffy, Kathryn.
II. Title.

PZ7.B74814Ei 2009
[Fic]—dc22

                                                                2008026052

Eidi

1

The four children had been sitting there waiting for a long time. But there was still nothing to be heard except the gurgling of the brook and the scouring of the pebbles on the shore as they were washed out to sea by the waters of the brook, then back to the shore by the waves.

A shrill cry rang out high above their heads, and they all looked up. An eagle was hovering over the sea on widespread wings.

The cry had set the heart of one of the girls beating wildly, and she laid her hand over it as if to calm it. Her light-brown eyes followed the eagle until it disappeared in the rays of the sun, which were slanting low over the face of the sea.

Her hair was plaited in a red-gold braid that ended in a curl in the middle of her back. A small scar showed white in one of her eyebrows.

She was tired of waiting. It shouldn't take this long, she thought. But it could.

The girl sitting beside her was a couple of years older. Her hair was dark and straight, her nose large and curved. She was holding a little boy on her lap; he was asleep. His mouth was open, and his head rested on her shoulder. A thin trail of drool had trickled from his mouth down her dark-blue dress.

At the older girl's feet lay a wire-haired black mongrel. The dog had cocked one ear at the eagle's cry without opening her eyes, as if she knew that it wasn't the kind of sound she had to attend to.

The last of the lot was a big boy, almost a young man, the oldest of them all. He had bright blue eyes and rather long dark hair, which was constantly falling in his eyes so that he had to keep brushing it aside. He sat whittling on a stick, and he'd been at it so long that there was quite a heap of shavings between his feet.

The children were sitting on the rocks above a cove in which there were three whitewashed houses. Thick smoke rose from one of the chimneys, though it had been a warm summer day. A flock of chickens were pecking around in front of the house, and on the grassy slope behind it various-colored sheep—black and gray, white and brown—could be seen.

A shout was heard from the cove below. A man had come to the doorway and stood there, calling, "Eidi! Ravnar! Myna! Doup!"

The children got to their feet and scrambled down the steep, rocky slope. First came Myna with Doup in her arms, though he was getting much too big to be carried around, and with the dog at her heels. After her came Ravnar, with his knife dangling from one hand and his stick in the other. Then came Eidi with lagging steps. Her leg had gone to sleep, and she was afraid she might stumble.

She was the last one to step through the door.

So that was what a newborn baby looked like. Little, red, and wrinkled, with small, half-dried blood clots in the fair hairs on its head. With white fat like congealed tallow in all its folds and creases. It lay there at Foula's breast like a pale little frog. It was wailing hoarsely, all four limbs sprawling.

They were allowed just one quick look at the naked baby. Then Foula tucked it under the blanket and gathered it close in to her. Her eyes shone up at Frid.

"Does it hurt, Mother?" asked Eidi. She had seen the ewes lambing.

Foula smiled at her and stroked her cheek with the back of her hand.

"Not anymore," she said. "And besides, what does it matter if it hurts a bit, when we've got such a lovely little boy."

"A boy!" exclaimed Eidi in surprise. "I thought it would be a girl, like me!"

"A little baby," marveled Doup, looking up at Myna, who nodded and smiled at him.

"Would you like to see him again?" asked Frid.

Doup nodded, and his father lifted him up so he could get a better view of his new half brother.

Ravnar, Frid's other son, stroked the little cheek gingerly with one finger, and Myna was allowed to hold the baby in her shawl for a moment. She stood quite still, gazing down into a pair of deep-blue eyes.

"It's like looking into the sky," she said.

Eidi turned away and walked out of the room and out of the house. She went right down to the edge of the sea and stood there staring over the water at the setting sun until black specks began to dance before her eyes and she had to look away from the glowing light.

She walked barefoot along the shore's edge over the small, round pebbles and felt how the water cooled her feet and the tears cooled her burning cheeks.

At last she came to where a big, flat rock jutted up in the shallow water near the shore. She waded out and climbed onto it. The waves lapped around the rock and sucked back with a sigh as they left the deep crannies in its sides. Little terns with pointed wings drew sharp angles across the orange sky. The sea smelled of salt and seaweed.

Eidi caught a tear on the tip of her tongue. It tasted of seawater. Then she wiped her eyes and her cheeks with the back of her hand, drew a deep breath, and stopped crying.

Now she could feel that she wasn't only sad but also relieved and glad. It had all gone well. Her mother was lying there smiling in her bed with a living child in her arms, and that was what counted.

The sun had gone down. It stayed hidden for a short while, only to appear again like a red full moon above the crest of the eastern hills, with a little star for company.

The evening was mild. All the same, there was a fire blazing on the hearth when she stepped into the main room. Foula was sitting on the settle bed with the new baby in her arms. The others were at the table having their supper.

The fire crackled, and Foula hummed bits of a melody now and again. The baby boy made small noises.

When they had eaten, Myna rose and got ready to go home to her own house. Doup wanted to go with her, and Ravnar went along to see them home. Eidi brought a chair and sat down by the settle bed. The baby boy had fallen asleep. He lay quite still, with his tiny hand clutching the edge of the blanket. His fingernails were so small that Eidi could hardly see them in the dim light.

"May I hold him?" she asked.

"I think you'd better wait a bit," said Foula. "He's sleeping now."

It was as though this new little creature gradually calmed everything in the room. Even the fire had ceased crackling, and let its flames lick soundlessly along the logs.

Foula had stopped humming; Frid sat very still at the table, looking at her and the child.

It was Foula who broke the silence.

"What shall we call him?"

"Cam," Eidi said after a while, "because everything goes calm and quiet around him."

"Cam," said Foula, considering.

The baby let go of the blanket and moved his arms; he seemed to be swimming up from the depths of sleep toward waking life before he opened his eyes.

He looked at Eidi, and she looked back at him, feeling that she was being regarded from another world.

"Cam," she called quietly.

And he answered her with a little squeak.

"Cam. It's a good name," she heard Frid say.

Foula nodded, and that was his name from then on.

2

Eidi had brought out the basket of cloth scraps. It held little pieces that had been left over from when they had sewn jackets, trousers, dresses, and skirts from the cloth they had woven last winter.

She sat down at the table by the window in order to see the different colors and patterns in a better light. Then she cut squares from each piece of cloth and laid them out side by side.

The rain beat on the windowpanes. Someone rattled the door latch. It was Myna coming over from her house. She came into the room with Doup at her heels. She had pulled her big gray shawl over her head, and now she took it off and shook it over the floor out in the passage.

"Such weather!" came Foula's voice from the hearth. "Did you see anything of Frid and Ravnar?"

"Are they out hunting?" Myna asked.

Foula nodded.

"I didn't see them," said Myna, and sat down at the table across from Eidi.

Doup climbed onto Myna's lap. She helped him out of his wet jacket.

"Oof, how wet we are."

Doup nodded. "It's raining," he said.

Foula brought a towel and gave it to Myna, who began to rub Doup's wet hair.

Foula stood by the table looking at Eidi's cloth squares.

"Are you making a better-luck-next-time?"

"What is that?" asked Myna, startled.

"Don't you know?" asked Foula. "They're also called try-your-lucks. It's a kind of shawl girls make for themselves when they want to find work. They use them to show how skillful they are at weaving, and how many different patterns they know."

Cam whimpered in his cradle, and Foula went back to him.

"Are you looking for work?" Myna asked Eidi, who shook her head.

"Ah no," she said. "I just felt like making one of those shawls."

Eidi worked on the shawl for several days. She crocheted all the squares together with dark-brown yarn. She trimmed the edges to make it three-cornered, and finished it off with a broad crocheted border all the way around. It had become a shawl with the colors of rocks and seafoam, of clouds and earth and the wet autumn heath.

She laid the shawl away under the seat of her settle bed, and then she began to knit a head scarf. This was also divided into squares showing all the different stitches she knew.

"That's a good idea," said Foula. "Not that you have any need to show your skills, but it makes a handsome scarf."

Eidi nodded, trying to thread the needle to tuck in the yarn ends. It was hard to see, even though she was sitting by the window. The panes were misted with vapor, and the air was hot and muggy from all the wash hanging on a line in front of the fire. The baby's knitted pants and undershirts and diaper cloths were ever present, hung up on the line and then taken down again as soon as they were dry to make room for the next clean, wet batch that was always waiting.

Summer was over, and the weather was often rainy. The harvest was gathered in, and they wouldn't be going hungry. The house, which Frid and Ravnar had repaired and lived in before Frid and Foula agreed to set up housekeeping there together, was full to bulging with potatoes, carrots, parsnips, and sacks of oats. The kale stalks stood in long ranks in the field behind the stone wall, where the sheep couldn't get at them. The hens had hatched out lots of chicks, and Myna's dog, Glennie, had kept the foxes off them, so most had survived.

And there were still mussels in the sea and sea kale along the shore, as there had been when Myna lived alone in Crow Cove with her grandmother. It was when her grandmother died that Myna had set off on her own, met all the others in her travels, and persuaded them to move here.

All except for the shepherd Rossan. He had

stayed in his little house on the heath with his sheep and his dogs.

Finally Eidi had fastened the last yarn end. The scarf was finished, and she laid it away in the settle bed with the shawl.

Eidi woke before sunrise. She sat up in the slate-gray twilight that was seeping through the windows and listened for what had woken her.

It couldn't have been Cam, because he and Frid and Foula slept in the room at the other end of the house, separated from this living room by the staircase up to the loft. Ravnar slept up there beside the warm chimney in a fishnet hammock.

Neither could it have been the logs on the fire crackling, because the embers had been banked with ashes to last the night, and the fireplace was only a black square in a dark-gray wall.

The mice hadn't begun to invade the house yet; they were still busy with the few remaining oats out in the fields.

Then she heard the sea. It couldn't be a storm, because there was no wind to be heard, but it did sound like swells beating on the shore. Or maybe it was just that waves sound louder in the last stillness of the night before the dawn.

Eidi got out of her settle bed and put on her clothes. When she stepped outside, she could see everything plainly in the dawn twilight, but it was all gray. The houses were light gray, the roofs dark gray, the sky overcast, without a star. It was a world where color didn't exist. She sat down on the stone steps and waited, without knowing what she was waiting for.

Then suddenly the slope behind Myna's house began to take on a greenish tinge, and the white-washed walls grew lighter and lighter until they were blindingly white against the green grass.

Eidi turned her head and saw that the sun, which was just peeping over the crest of the hill, had found a hole in the ceiling of cloud. Through this hole it was sending a cone of light over Crow Cove, bringing color back to the world.

Then all at once it was over. The clouds closed again, and when the others in the house got up, it was an ordinary gray day with muted colors, like any other. But not for Eidi.

That evening she told Foula and Frid that she had decided to go back to Rossan and ask him if he needed help with the wool from all his sheep. If he did, then she would stay the winter there and card and spin it for him, in readiness for the big spring market.

"You're too young to make your own way in the world," said Foula.

Eidi shook her head. "I've already been out in the world," she said.

"Yes, but you had me with you."

"Ravnar could go with me," Eidi suggested.

So that was how it was.

3

Eidi turned at the top of the hill and looked back one last time at the cove.

She hadn't been this far along the inland path since the first time she and Foula had walked here with Doup and Myna. She had forgotten how small the houses looked from up here. Little white building blocks around a thread of a brook so small that she could barely make it out. Though she knew it was really so deep that you got your legs wet above the knees if you waded across instead of crossing on the bridge.

"You're in an awful hurry," said Ravnar, catching up with her at last.

Eidi smiled at him.

"Sorry. I didn't know I could walk faster than you."

They followed the path for several hours, over stony ridges and down into damp hollows where their shoes got soaked and every step made a slurping sound.

When at last they reached the big stone by the high road, it was Ravnar who had to wait for Eidi.

When she caught up with him, they sat down with their backs to the stone and opened the bag of provisions Foula had given them.

The sun had come out. It warmed the stone they were leaning against. They carefully peeled off the ashy gray skins of the baked potatoes and ate them with slices of smoked mutton.

"Why do you want to leave?" asked Ravnar after a while.

Eidi shrugged. "I don't know," she said. "There didn't seem to be enough room."

"There are houses enough there," Ravnar objected.

"That's not the way I meant."

"I guess I know what you mean," Ravnar said. "Something about Frid and Foula having enough in each other and their little Cam, with no room for anyone else."

The last bite of potato seemed to swell up in Eidi's mouth. She swallowed it with difficulty and nodded. Ravnar hastily wiped his knife on a wisp of grass and stuck it in his belt. Then he got to his feet and slung the haversack onto his shoulder. Eidi picked up her bundle, and they went on together.

For several days they walked in the still, cool air, seeing no movement other than the traveling wedges of migrating birds above their heads.

Although summer was over, the grass was still green. But the sky was no longer deep blue. It was as if the chilly air had washed nearly all the color out of it, and ragged white mists did their best to veil what little color was left.

Eidi shivered beneath her shawl, though there was no breath of wind. It was as if the world was waiting with bated breath. The sound of their foot-steps was distinct on the stony road. Every once in a while she started to sing, only to fall silent after a few verses. Her voice sounded so little in such a wide world that it seemed better to keep still.

Once, the toe of her shoe caught a stone and

sent it skimming down the road, and she started violently in fear. At that she defied the silence and burst into song at the top of her voice. But no matter how loud she sang, the stillness drained her voice away and made it as thin as the pale blue of the sky.

Then, as they came around a bend in the road, there lay Rossan's house out on the heath. Light-gray smoke was curling up from the chimney in neat spirals.

Eidi began to run hard, but she couldn't keep going at that pace, so Ravnar overtook her, and together they turned onto the path that led to the house.

Rossan's black wire-haired dog, who was lying on the stone step, uttered a single bark, then rose and came to meet them. When she caught Eidi's scent, she started wagging her whole back end. Eidi patted old Glennie's graying head very gently.

Another dog stuck its head through the doorway. This one looked exactly like Myna's dog, except for the little white fan that Myna's young Glennie had on her chest. They were sisters, and the old dog was their mother. As soon as the young dog saw why the old one had barked, she shot down the path like an arrow. When she reached them, she didn't wag her tail but kept a wary distance. She didn't remember Eidi, and she had never met Ravnar.

Then a boy stuck his head out the door. He was a bit taller than Eidi, and his hair was so fair it was white, and it stuck straight out all over.

"Hey!" he shouted. "Who are you?"

By this time they were almost at the house, and now Rossan appeared in the doorway.

"Why, if it isn't Eidi and Ravnar! Welcome, welcome!"

Rossan came down the steps, smiling widely. He clapped Ravnar on the shoulder and gave Eidi a hug.

His gray hair was as trim and smooth as ever under his knitted cap, but his bearded face was as wrinkled as willow bark, and Eidi saw suddenly how the passing time had made him older and made her bigger. Her head reached nearly to his chin.

"And this is Kotka, my sister's boy."

Kotka stepped forward and shook hands politely. Eidi noticed that his eyes were bright and blue, and his hand warm and dry.

"What's this?" said Rossan, looking at her shawl. "Are you out to try your luck, Eidi?"

Eidi nodded and said, "Yes. I thought I might try it with you."

Rossan laughed. "Why, you don't need a shawl for that. I know how good your work is. But I like your way of going about it. You do the thing properly while you're at it. You're hired."

So Rossan hadn't forgotten the fine yarn Eidi and Foula had spun for him that winter when they, along with Myna and Doup, had stayed with him.

"But come in! Kotka, put the soup back over the fire. You two must be tired of journey rations and cold food."

The house was very small. It consisted of only one room, with a steep stair up to the attic. Eidi looked around the cozy room where she had sat day after day carding wool while Foula spun it on the spinning wheel in the corner.

Rossan had slept up in the attic then, and the others below in the living room. But this time it would be different.

"I'll sleep in the attic," said Eidi.

"Aha, so you've decided that already."

Eidi nodded.

"Well then, we'll have to let you have your way.

And what about you, Ravnar? Are you looking for a place as well?"

Ravnar shook his head.

"No, I just came along to keep Eidi company on the way. I'll be heading back tomorrow. We'll start butchering as soon as I get home."

In a short while they were sitting at the little table. The soup was hot and chock-full of herbs and pieces of meat. The surface was delicately pearled with fat, and the aroma of it made Eidi's stomach growl. They hadn't had anything to eat yesterday. The journey had taken longer than they had reckoned on.

4

Eidi took a deep breath as Ravnar's dark head disappeared from sight around the bend of the road. Now at last she was all alone in the big world, without anyone from home in Crow Cove. And before long she would be even farther away. Kotka had come to tend the sheep while Rossan took his wool to the autumn market.

Rossan had so much wool that Eidi wouldn't be able to spin it all into yarn even if she worked the entire winter. So although she was here now, Rossan still intended to make the trip and sell some of the wool, and she was to go with him.

They would follow the little track that ran by Rossan's house, across the heath and up over the gray range of hills that could just be glimpsed far away. Beyond that lay Eastern Harbor, a big seaport town, where you could get a good price for your wares. Trading ships put in there from faraway places, eager to buy and sell.

That was where Kotka lived with his mother, Rossan's sister Lesna, and they could stay with her during the market season.

Fortunately they had Lesna's horse, which Kotka had ridden over. It couldn't carry them both, but at least it could carry the wool, so they wouldn't have to lug it on their own backs.

Big bales of wool were brought down from the loft and tied to the horse's back, together with a blanket for each of them, because the nights could be cold in the hills. Finally they strapped their haversack on top and started on their journey.

The track wound in and out between willow scrub and bogholes. These were almost indiscernible, their surfaces green with moss and tussocks.

"Mind you, don't step off the path," warned Rossan.

So Eidi trudged carefully along behind him and the horse.

"Once you fall in there," he went on, "no one can get you out again. You just get sucked down, like Myna's sheep did."

"And Doup and Ravnar's mother," Eidi added.

"Oh yes," said Rossan over his shoulder. "That was a sad thing, to die like that."

Rossan sighed again. After a little while he went on: "But Frid and your mother have each other now, and they've even got a new little boy. So everyone's happy, aren't they?"

"Not me," said Eidi.

"Goodness me," said Rossan mildly. "So you reckon there were too many chicks in the nest, do you?"

Eidi nodded.

"I think you'd better make up your mind to love him. Otherwise he'll get to be like a stone in your shoe that you can't shake out, just a constant annoyance."

Eidi didn't answer. She didn't want to hear any more.

Day by day they climbed higher. Now the bogs were few and far between. Heather, gorse and bog myrtle, scrub oak and willow flanked the path on either side. Shallow creeks trickled among the stones and formed small, clear pools, where black bugs skimmed across the surface on long, thin legs.

At last they reached the top of the ridge. Here the wind from the west, north, and east had worn away all the vegetation, so the rock face lay scrubbed and bare. Only a few tufts of grass survived in south-facing crevices and dells. Boulders jutted up like the backs of big gray animals resting on little green paws.

They'd had good weather so far, but up here a cold wind was on the prowl. It made Eidi dig out her head scarf and wrap her shawl tighter around her. Rossan's breathing grew labored.

"It's a good thing it'll soon be downhill the rest of the way," he said after a while, as they rested and warmed themselves in a south-facing stony dell.

The sun was going down. It would be a cold night.

"Maybe we should camp here," said Rossan.

"There's a lot of heat from the sun in this rock. It won't turn cold in one night."

Eidi looked at him. "Yes, let's do that," she said. He seemed tired.

The country was spread out at their feet, an erratic pattern of brown and gray, green and blue, with here and there a little white block of a house, to remind them that there were still other people in the world.

They unloaded the wool, blankets, and haversacks from the horse. The wind was too strong to let them light a fire, so they made do with a supper of cold mutton and a couple of onions that they had roasted in their skins in the embers of last night's fire.

Mountain ranges of clouds formed on the horizon. The sun sank behind them. Darkness fell, and the wind rose. It found a crack to howl in and, as if egged on by the sound of its own voice, blew more and more wildly.

"Better tether the horse," said Rossan.

They usually let the horse go free, so he could graze in the early mornings before they set out.

As Eidi got to her feet, a raindrop struck her

face, and in the next breath the rain came beating down. With the rain came darkness. She couldn't see a thing. The wind blew in sudden gusts from all quarters, and she could hardly keep her balance. Then came a flash of lightning that lit up the terrain near and far, and she caught a glimpse of the horse, standing on the rocky overhang right above their heads.

A clap of thunder rent the air, and the horse's hooves scrambled across the stony ground. Then came an alarming scraping sound and the clatter of falling rocks. The next flash of lightning showed her Rossan stretched out on the ground with a bleeding wound over one eye. She reached him just as the thunder crashed over them.

"Rossan!" she called, but he didn't answer.

She fumbled for the water flask to wash the wound, but the next lightning flash showed her there was no need for that. The rain was washing the blood from his forehead in a steady trickle onto the ground.

A blanket, she thought, and groped along the rock face for their belongings. She found a blanket, brought it back, and covered him with it, but before long she realized that it wouldn't be enough to keep him warm in this ice-cold rain. It was already soaking wet.

Then she thought of the wool. The raw, oily wool that could keep a sheep warm and safe through the rainiest winter. She got hold of a bale and dragged it over to Rossan's unconscious form. But there was still the wind. How could she keep the wind from tearing the wool away?

Then she had an idea. She spread the blanket out as far as it would go, weighting down the edges with heavy stones as she went. She left a loose corner at the top and began to stuff wool in under the blanket. She used the whole bale, and when she was through, Rossan's little potbelly swelled the blanket like an enormous paunch. He was packed in wool from his toes right up to his ears. She even stuffed wool in his knitted cap and pulled it down over his forehead, right to the edge of the wound.

At last she crept in between the packed-in wool and the blanket, wrapped in her scarf, her shawl, and the other blanket, and fell into an exhausted sleep next to Rossan while the rain lashed the bare rocks and the thunder drew away into the distance.

5

Someone was moving. Someone or other was making mumbling noises. Eidi opened her eyes.

For a moment she didn't know who or where she was. All she knew was that something had woken her. Then she recalled what had happened last night. Next it dawned on her that the storm was over. She sat up with a start and looked at Rossan.

He was the one who had moved. He had lifted his hand to his forehead in his sleep, and when he touched the sore place he mumbled to himself. His eyes flew open, and he looked around dazedly.

"What happened?" he asked faintly.

"You got hit on the head with a stone. The horse started a little rockslide when he was scared by the lightning. He ran off."

Just then they heard a soft whicker above their heads. Eidi glanced up. There stood Lesna's horse looking down at them.

"See there, he's come back!" she cried.

"That's a lucky thing," mumbled Rossan, as though he was still not entirely sure what was going on.

"Look here, what have you done to me?" he asked, peering bemusedly down the length of his enormous body.

He stuck his hand in under the blanket and began pulling out wool in big tufts. Then he started to laugh.

"Well, I never!" He chuckled. "Where did you get that idea?"

"From the sheep," answered Eidi. "That's how they keep warm, after all."

And Rossan laughed again.

"Yes indeed, an old sheep, that's me . . . all over!" he declared.

He struggled out of the blanket and got to his feet, but he was dizzy and almost fell over.

"I guess it was a bad bump," he said, and sat back down hurriedly.

Eidi packed the wool into a bale again, fetched the horse, and loaded their things on his back. Then she sat down beside Rossan.

"How far do we still have to go?" she asked.

"We should be able to see the town from here, maybe from just over the ridge."

"Do you think you can make it?"

Rossan nodded. "If we rest every now and then," he said.

So they set off again.

Eidi had never seen a big town. The rocky cliffs formed a natural harbor, a bay that widened out once you were past the harbor mouth. The houses were clustered along the steep surrounding slopes. What she couldn't get over was the noise of the gulls. The air was thick with them. Their screams drowned out every other sound. They hurt Eidi's ears.

Rossan leaned heavily on her shoulder as they made their way through the narrow streets.

"We have to get up there," he panted, pointing to a white house at the top of the steepest slope along the right side of the bay.

Step by step they labored up the street. The horse had taken the lead. He knew the way, and Eidi felt that the only thing that kept her on her feet and moving was that she could cling to his bridle.

She had tears of exertion in her eyes, and her legs were trembling under her. Just as they reached the gate of the house, Rossan collapsed, and Eidi couldn't get him to his feet. She had let go of the bridle, and the horse immediately deserted them and made for the back of the house.

Then the front door opened, and a woman came running down the garden path and straight to Rossan. She bent over him but couldn't rouse him.

"What's happened to him?" she asked.

"He got hit on the head by a rockslide. He could hardly walk the last bit up here."

"Come!" said the woman. "We must get him to bed."

She got a grip under his armpits, and Eidi took hold of his legs, but they couldn't lift him. So they each took a grip under an armpit and dragged him all the way into the house and over the threshold of the big room at the end. Together they managed to bundle him onto the bed there. The woman undressed him and tucked him up under the covers. Then she sat down on a chair to get her breath.

Her hair was just as white as Kotka's, though whether that was from age or because she was so fair, Eidi couldn't tell.

The woman was younger than Rossan, leaner and more sharp-featured. She was wearing a handsome lavender-blue dress with a big white apron over it.

She sat looking at Eidi for a little while, as if to determine what sort of person she was, before giving a hand in greeting. Eidi told her who she was, why she had come along with Rossan, and what had happened.

Just then the bedclothes rustled. Rossan was coming to.

"Here's a pretty state of things," Lesna said to him. "A good thing the horse came back. I don't know what I'd have done without him. Now you'd better stay where you are until you're properly rested, and I'll put the horse in the stable and tend to him, and get this child a bite to eat."

Even in his worn-out state, Rossan managed to send Eidi a little smile from the bed.

She wasn't a child. She was out to earn her living, not just tagging along as a burden.

The smoked herring fillets were warm; the scrambled eggs were rich yellow and soft, sprinkled with finely chopped chives; the butter was spread thick on the bread; and the tea was hot and sweet.

Eidi ate alone at the table while Lesna served her. She had three helpings. Afterward Lesna showed her to a little room by the stable where she was to sleep.

A settle bed stood open and pulled out, made up with white, smooth linen. The whitewashed walls hadn't a damp patch on them, and the floor was swept and scrubbed. But it was cold, dreadfully cold, and Eidi's sore and weary body could find no rest until it occurred to her to open the inner door to the stable, where the horse lived, to let some of that comforting warmth in.

Every time she closed her eyes she saw the white gulls diving at her with loud, hoarse, screaming cries—until the horse's comfortable munching and rustling drove their calls away and brought peace to her ears.

6

Rossan was too weak to go to market. So he considered getting someone else to sell his wool for him, but that would mean a lower price. The man who did the selling would need to have something for his trouble as well.

But Eidi had already decided that she would sell the wool for him.

"You don't know anything about dickering," said Rossan, shaking his head.

"Dickering?" asked Eidi, puzzled.

"Yes, dickering on the price. First you name a price that's higher than what you want to get. Then the buyer names a price that is less than he's willing to pay. Then you lower your price a trifle, and the buyer raises his, until you meet somewhere in the middle. That's dickering."

"Aha," said Eidi. "I guess I can learn to do that."

So Rossan started playing the part of a customer. He was a very good complainer.

"That bale is full of sheep dung! Just look at all that muck! And you're asking money for that, something anybody could pick up in a field? If they'd touch it, that is. Maybe you only shear the back legs. Where do you keep your clean wool, pray tell?"

Then it was Eidi's turn.

"You're right, it's not as clean as it might be," she said confidingly, and took a bit off the price.

Rossan laughed.

"That was a good one! You'll manage just fine."

So Eidi was allowed to take the wool to market.

The market was held on a big green on the other side of the road along the harbor.

Eidi had a booth down by the shore, alongside someone Lesna knew, a fat woman selling knitted sweaters. Lesna helped Eidi load the wool onto the horse. She went with her to the marketplace and led the horse home again when they had unloaded the bales.

When Lesna had gone, Eidi sat down on one of the bales and looked around her in wonder. There were a lot of people selling wool and yarn, woven cloth and knitted garments, but there were booths with all sorts of other things as well.

"Go on, take a walk around and see the sights," said the woman to Eidi, knitting all the while, as though her hands went on working by themselves and were no concern of hers. "I'll keep an eye on your wool."

There were silken shawls with long, sleek fringes; there were hair ribbons and peacocks' feathers. There were gold belt buckles, and buttons of silver and bone and mother-of-pearl.

There was tea and sugar and tobacco, salt and flour and oatmeal, dried apples and prunes and raisins, fragrant spices and great bunches of thyme.

There were potatoes and cabbages, carrots and onions, parsnips and leeks. There was dried fish by the bundle and salt fish in barrels and smoked bacon and big loaves of bread and pots of butter and honey cakes and . . .

Eidi was reminded of the food Lesna had packed for her, and even though it was much too early, she hurried back to her booth to unpack it.

A man was standing by the booth. "Are you here to sell your wares or just to amuse yourself?" he snapped as she approached.

"To sell, sir," she hastened to say.

"None of that, now, Bandon," said the woman in the next booth. "The girl has to have a chance to look about a little. Don't you remember when you were a little lad at your first market?"

But it seemed the man didn't want to remember being any smaller than he was now. And now he was big—both tall and wide, and his thick, fur-trimmed coat and the fur hat on his head made him look even bigger.

"Mind your own business," he said stiffly to the woman, turned on his heel, and walked off.

"Oh no!" exclaimed Eidi.

"Never you mind," said the woman. "He'll be back. Your wool is the best in the market, and he knows what he wants. So hold fast to your price!"

"Who is he?"

"Bandon? He's the richest man in town. He has a finger in every pie, deals in every kind of goods, and thinks he runs the whole show. But once upon a time he was a snotty-nosed little tyke who got kicked out too early, because his mother, who was a widow, married a shopkeeper who didn't care for any youngsters but his own.

"And even though they've both been dead for years, he still wants to show them what a big man he's made of himself. He hangs around the fine folk, and us that knew him in the old days? Why, he won't let on he ever saw us before. He's puffing himself up, so he is, and one day he's going to burst with a bang," she concluded.

The woman was right. Bandon returned while Eidi was looking after both booths to give her neighbor a break.

He poked a bale with his stick. "Tell me, do you just shear the back ends of the beasts?" he said.

"No, sir," answered Eidi politely. "We shear the whole sheep."

"So where do you keep the clean wool?"

Eidi couldn't help smiling.

"Right here," she said, and dragged out a bale of white wool.

"Are you mocking me?"

"No, sir. I just meant that it might be easier for you to see how clean the wool is when it's white."

Bandon growled, and the bargaining began. Eidi had to struggle to stand fast and not be put upon, but she kept up her end and got very nearly the price she had determined on. Bandon bought the white bale first and then a light-brown one. He paid her and left the bales with her. Someone would come and fetch them later, he said.

"Well done," said the knitting woman when she came back and heard all about it. Shortly after that, a slight young boy turned up and inquired after the wool.

"Why, you can't lug even one of those bales by yourself," Eidi protested. "I'd better give you a hand."

But the woman made signs to her not to, so Eidi had to be content with hoisting it up for him to get hold of.

"Bandon would never forgive him if he should see that he can't manage by himself," the woman explained when the boy had left. "He's so hard on that lad!"

"Who is he?"

"He's the son of a woman Bandon took into his house. But Bandon's not his father, because she was already with child when they met. She died in childbirth, and then Bandon kept the boy."

The boy returned shortly for the other bale. Despite the cold wind, his forehead was wet with sweat.

"Sit down awhile," the woman said kindly. The boy shook his head.

"Oh, come now," said Eidi. "Just for a minute. I'll get you a mug of tea."

And before he could answer, she had darted over to the tea booth and bought mugs of tea for all three of them.

The boy glanced around him nervously before he took the mug.

"Just you tell him that you've been drinking tea with his old sweetheart," said the woman with a laugh. "That ought to shut him up."

The boy looked at her in amazement.

"Yes, you may believe it or not, but even Bandon was young and handsome once, with brown, curly hair and fair cheeks and a red, kissable mouth. Oh, weren't the girls all after him! But now he's getting old and bad-tempered. And never mind about the first part of that—we all get old—but the second part no one wants to put up with."

At that moment a bellow was heard across the marketplace. Bandon had spotted the boy.

"Get away from those slatterns and get a move on!" he yelled, and the boy started up, the mug smashing on the stones while the tea splashed his trouser leg.

"Leave it, I'll take care of it," said the woman, picking up the pieces. Eidi lifted the bale, and the boy staggered off with his burden.

7

In the few days the market lasted, Eidi sold all the wool. On the last day, Rossan gave her some money to buy something for herself before all the booths were packed up.

She went from booth to booth, having trouble deciding, until she saw a row of mother-of-pearl buttons fastened onto a little piece of cloth. They weren't just white, like ordinary buttons; they glowed with many different hues.

Then she caught sight of a mussel shell, lying on display among the buttons. It was as big as her hand, and grayish brown and drab on the outside. But the inside gleamed with the same shifting colors as the buttons: green and blue, silver and white.

"How much does that cost?" she asked.

She held out her coins, and the man shot them a quick glance.

"More than you can afford. I have one that's chipped a bit. You can have that for what you've got there."

But Eidi did some dickering, and in the end she left the booth with the chipped shell and half the mother-of-pearl buttons.

Dusk was falling, and the screams of the gulls were at last silenced. People were packing up. Some were sitting drinking around a fire they had made in an old iron pot. Eidi started up the hill toward Lesna's house.

There were still crowds of people down by the harbor, but higher up, the streets and alleys were deserted. Suddenly Eidi heard a scream. She stopped and listened. Someone was crying out for help, and Eidi ran toward the sound.

Across from her on a narrow street, in front of a row of houses, stood a man with a bottle in his hand. Facing him stood the woman who had shouted. She was holding her cheek with one hand while the other was raised to protect her head.

The man lifted his empty hand to strike again.

"No!" Eidi yelled, and plunged between them. Too late she saw that it was her former stepfather, the man she and Foula had fled from, the one who had given her the scar on her eyebrow.

The blow struck Eidi with such force that she was thrown off her feet and landed on the slippery cobblestones some way off.

A ringing sound gathered inside her, as if she had an iron pot over her head. The sound turned into a white-hot ball that exploded in thousands of stars forcing their way outward at a raging speed. She felt that she was being pierced by a thousand needles. Then darkness closed down, the pain came to a point on the side of her head, and the sound turned to a shrill, constant howl.

Eidi whimpered softly.

"I'm sorry," she heard a woman's voice say above her.

Then the woman's voice was farther away. "Let's get out of here. You could have killed her." A voice blurred with drink mumbled something about guttersnipes and wenches not interfering with a man, and Eidi realized that he hadn't recognized her.

The footsteps faded away, a bottle smashed somewhere around a corner, and then everything was quiet. And in the stillness Eidi became aware that the howling tone came from inside her ear.

Her jaw hurt horribly, her knees and hands and cheeks were raw with grazes from the hard cobbles, and she had lost her mussel shell and the mother-of-pearl buttons.

She crawled around on her knees to look for them. Something shiny caught her eye over by the wall of a house. The pale moonlight escaping for a moment from the clouds picked it out. It was a piece of the shell. A little farther off she found the cloth with the buttons. Only one of them had survived being trodden on.

She took the fragment of shell and the button and limped up the street to Rossan and Lesna.

Rossan sat up in bed when she came into the room. "Well, did you find something you liked?" he asked.

Eidi stumbled across the room to the bed. She fell on her knees, buried her head in the covers, and sobbed. Her hands were clutching the mussel shell and the button.

Rossan took them from her and laid them gently on the chest of drawers beside the bed. He stroked her hair.

"There, there," he said. "Did you fall in the dark? That's a nasty steep street out there. And your nice things all broken!" He was talking to her as if she were a little child, but she didn't mind. Not now, and not since it was Rossan. And she cried like a little child, long and heartily.

At last her weeping grew quieter, and she lifted her head and wiped her eyes with the backs of her hands.

"For goodness' sake! Just look at you!" exclaimed Rossan. He called out for his sister. While Lesna was cleaning her cuts and scrapes, Eidi told them what had happened.

"That man just can't take the drink," said Rossan, shaking his head, "and he keeps on drinking more and more. Keep well away from him! If he discovers who you are, he might start asking around about Foula and looking for her again."

Later, as Eidi lay in her room by the stable, her

ear was still howling, but the comfortable rustling sounds from the horse in his stall held the noise at bay, and she soon fell asleep.

The next morning she had forgotten all about the weird noise. She was on her way down to the harbor with an empty pail. Lesna had seen a fishing boat putting in and she wanted Eidi to buy a couple of flounders.

Just as she was about to step onto the green where the market had been held, Eidi heard the howling in her ear again. She stopped in surprise and shook her head, like a horse plagued by a horsefly, and just then her stepfather and the woman he was with came walking across the green and disappeared between the houses on the far side. Then the howling noise stopped. It was as if it had sounded just to warn her.

When Eidi got back, Rossan was sitting in the sunshine on a bench in front of the house. He was recovering slowly, but he had begun to get up now and then.

The wind had fallen, so the sun felt warm. The

last roses were blooming against the housefront. Eidi sat down beside him and started cleaning the fish. Lesna's cat took charge of the offal and kept the gulls at a distance.

The sea was blue and smooth. Little gray boats with empty sails and full holds lay offshore waiting for a breath of wind. The fragrance of sun-warmed thyme and sage mingled with the salty smell of fish and blood and the smoke from Rossan's pipe. The cat crunched on fish heads and tails, and through the open window they could hear Lesna rattling pots and pans.

"I'm going to look for work," said Eidi. "I should pay Lesna something for food."

"You don't need to do that," said Rossan. "We'll be leaving just as soon as I'm well enough. I'm going to buy a horse with the money you got for the wool, and Lesna will let us take hers along for Kotka to ride back on, so the trip home won't be so long or so hard."

"I'm eating Lesna out of house and home," Eidi protested.

Rossan laughed. "She can just stop cooking so well. That's what I'm always telling her when she complains about Kotka's appetite. And I gave her a bit of money for our keep, so you don't owe her anything."

"But then I owe you."

He shook his head and smiled at her. "Don't fret. There'll be time enough for all that and more. You have a whole, long life ahead of you."

8

Eidi didn't need to look for work. It came to her.

"You there—girl with the shawl—you from the market!" she heard a familiar voice calling behind her the next morning as she was going to buy tobacco for Rossan.

She turned around, and there stood Bandon in his hat and coat, although the autumn afternoon was turning warm.

"My name is Eidi," she said stiffly, because now that she had no more wool to sell, she didn't need to be any more polite than she felt like.

"Miss Eidi," said Bandon in a sarcastic tone, but with the hint of a twinkle in his eye, "may I be permitted to ask if that shawl is your own handiwork, and if such is the case, if you might care to do some weaving for me?"

"Yes, I made it myself," she answered the first question.

"Very nice," said Bandon. "And if I'm not mistaken, one customarily wears such a shawl when one is seeking to be hired. Am I right?"

Eidi nodded.

"And that is why I am inquiring as to whether the young lady might be inclined to weave for me."

Eidi clutched the shawl closer around her. She didn't know what she should say. She did want to work, but she didn't like the way he had treated that boy.

"I pay good wages," he went on. "The little lady can live at home or at my house, just as she pleases. I provide board and lodging, or else I pay a higher wage if you provide those things for yourself. I will expect an answer about sundown today. You'll find me at home."

He doffed his fur hat to her, turned, and was gone.

Rossan didn't like the idea, but Lesna thought it was a good deal. "Bandon isn't a bad sort, really," she maintained. "And a big girl like you ought to turn her hand to something, so you can learn that no one gets food for nothing."

"If I don't live at Bandon's house," said Eidi, "he will pay higher wages. I've decided to say yes so Rossan won't have to pay you for us both."

Lesna nodded approvingly, got to her feet, and went out to the kitchen to start preparing a meat pie with sage.

At dusk Lesna went with Eidi to Bandon's big house on the edge of the green. It had a view of the sea, so he could keep an eye out for the ships that bought his wares or sold goods to him. Behind the house were the outbuildings, stables, and warehouses.

Lesna and Eidi were shown in by an old man whose back was so bent that his head was level with his shoulder blades. They found Bandon sitting in a big, high-ceilinged room behind a massive table.

"Why, it's you, Lesna," he said in surprise.

Eidi noticed that Lesna's features opened like a flower unfolding in the sun, while the faintest of blushes spread all the way up to the roots of her white hair.

Bandon had the old servant bring chairs for both of them. Eidi suspected that she would have had to remain standing if she had come alone.

"I thought you had only sons," said Bandon.

"Four in all," said Lesna, "and three of them grown. There's only Kotka left at home. Eidi here has a place with my brother, but he's too poorly for them to travel home just yet, so . . ."

"So," continued Eidi, "I would like to find some work to do just until we leave."

"Then why do you go around wearing that shawl, which indicates that you're looking for hire?"

"It's true, that isn't quite fair," Lesna said hastily, "when you already have a place with Rossan."

"But I do want a job," Eidi protested. "Otherwise I wouldn't be sitting here. Besides, it's the only shawl I brought with me," she added in a low voice.

In the end they agreed that Eidi would weave for Bandon as long as she stayed in town, and that she would go on boarding with Lesna.

Bandon escorted them to the door, nodded to Eidi, and kissed Lesna's hand.

"He's so courtly," Lesna exclaimed on the way across the green, and then the flower folded its petals, and her face became once again a bit sharp and tight, as usual.

Bandon's house hummed with life. The courtyard was always teeming with people. In the rear buildings there was a shop where people could buy anything they might otherwise have bought at the market. Only now it cost twice as much, because there were no other merchants to drive the price down. But people traded there all the same, because there was a lot to choose from at Bandon's all year round.

In the evening, though, the courtyard fell quiet. The sounds of voices and the clop of horses' hooves ceased, and all that was heard was an occasional deep bark from the watchdog and the rattle of his chain. Eidi worked right across the courtyard from the shop, in a half-cellar room with windows that gave her a good view of it.

She often worked late, because she was paid not by the hour but for every shawl she finished. The patterns and colors were up to her. Some of the shawls were square, others long with fringes at both ends, and they were sold as fast as she could weave them.

One evening the quiet was broken by Bandon's angry voice and the sobs of a child. Eidi looked out the window and saw in the dusk Bandon dragging the boy she had met at the market down the steps of the shop. At the foot of the steps he raised his hand, and Eidi was just about to dash out and thrust herself between them when her ear started to howl. She stopped in her tracks.

"I'll teach you to steal!" shouted Bandon, and gave the boy a resounding box on the ear.

Then Bandon turned on his heel and strode into the house. The boy sat down on the lowest step and hid his face in his hands, sobbing.

Eidi crept into the yard and went over to the boy. The watchdog growled but stayed lying where he was.

"Come with me," Eidi whispered. She took the boy's hand and helped him up, then led him into the weaving room.

His nose was bleeding. She made him tilt his head back and hold a wisp of wool to his nostrils.

"What happened?" she asked.

"He found out I'd been stealing raisins," the boy said, and hiccuped at the ceiling.

"Are you hungry?" she asked. He nodded.

She brought out the rest of the food Lesna had sent with her; she hadn't taken time to finish it.

She put lamb chops and bread and cheese on the table, and the boy began to devour it, still holding the tuft of wool to his nostrils.

"What's your name, by the way?" she asked.

"Hink," he muttered behind the wool with his mouth full.

"Hink?" she repeated.

He chewed what was in his mouth and blurted, "No. Tink!" before taking another bite.

He ate everything she had laid out. In the meantime, she packed her things together, and then they left the room. They gave the chop bones to the watchdog, who wagged his tail when Tink took them to him.

"Come and see me tomorrow," whispered Eidi before she slipped through the courtyard entryway toward home.

When she stepped into Lesna's living room, Rossan was sitting by the fireplace with a blanket over his knees, knitting a stocking. Lesna was patching a pair of Kotka's trousers.

"Well, how did it go today?" she asked.

Eidi was just about to tell them about Tink when a very faint sound, like the shrill hum of a mosquito on the way toward her ear, startled her and made her think again.

"Fine," she said. "I finished the brown shawl with the black stripe-check. I put alternating black and brown fringe on it."

"Sounds good. I hear round about that Bandon is pleased with you," said Lesna.

"And so he thundering well should be," muttered Rossan above the winking knitting needles.

9

The next evening, while Eidi was again sitting at work at Bandon's, she had a sudden impulse. She left the loom and crossed the courtyard to the main house, where she slipped through the little door to the kitchen.

The cook wasn't there. A single candle burned on the table. Eidi looked around and caught sight of another candlestick in the window, with a stump of candle in it. She took this and lit the stump with the candle on the table.

There were several doors off the kitchen. Behind one of them she heard the cook cough. That one must have led to the cook's room. Next came the door to the cellar. The darkness behind it smelled of mold and crumbling plaster. The next door was locked. It was very narrow and almost certainly opened onto the pantry, since a faint whiff of sausages and meat pie seeped through it. Behind the last door was a staircase to a long corridor half a floor up. She went along this, assuming that it led to Bandon's big room.

At the end of the passage she stopped in front of a heavy oak door. She knocked on it hesitantly. There was no answer. She waited for a moment and listened in the darkness. All was still. So she went in.

The room was very dimly lit by the glow from the fire. The chair behind the massive desk was empty. She went toward the fireplace and the two big leather chairs that stood with their backs toward her.

"Come and sit down," said Bandon's voice suddenly from beyond one of the chair backs.

It was as if he had been expecting her.

She drew nearer to the brown leather chairs. There he sat, running a finger around the edge of a fine, polished glass he held in his hand. A square decanter filled with a deep red liquid stood on a little table by his side.

She sat down gingerly in the empty chair and looked at him. His full red lips gleamed moistly against the dark-tinged, smooth-shaven jaw. He went on staring into the flames while he set the glass on the table, drew the stopper from the decanter, and refilled the glass to the brim.

"He had a nosebleed," she said.

"He did, eh," said Bandon without looking at her.

A spark flew out of the fire and landed on the stone floor almost at her feet. It blazed up a moment before it went out.

Bandon spoke again. "Most people tend to think that the colors you see in fire are yellow and red, maybe white, but nothing else. But that's because they haven't really looked. Look at that knot of wood over there in the corner of the stove. Can you see the green flame on the underside? In its innermost core it's as blue as a kingfisher's wing. I'm convinced that all the colors in the world can be found in burning things."

"I expect you're right," said Eidi.

She could feel the warmth of the fire making her stiff, tired body surrender. She leaned back in the chair and let her arms slide from the armrests onto her lap. They sat in silence for a while.

"They say I have a lot of children," Bandon began. "And it's probably true—the womenfolk used to like me when I was young. I don't know those children and I never have and I suppose I never shall. Fortunately or unfortunately, who's to tell. At any rate, they aren't troubled with a father who never wanted to be one. Or wanted to be a husband, for that matter. Except for once."

Eidi sat very still so as not to distract him. He had emptied his glass, and he filled it again before he went on.

"She came on a ship one day, when they were holding the market. She was alone, and anyone could see she was with child. She hadn't many wares to sell, and what she did sell were her last bits and pieces, all that she had. I bought the whole lot and offered to marry her. I had fallen in love with her the minute I saw her.

"I was so used to the girls wanting me that I couldn't imagine she would refuse me. She did, though; she said she didn't know me, which was fair enough. But I felt that I'd known her all my life.

"So I hired her as my cook. And I courted her as I've never courted anyone. And at last I got her consent. But she wanted to wait with the wedding until after she'd given birth."

Bandon stopped speaking and sat looking into the fire awhile; his finger began following the rim of the glass. Eidi noticed the broad gold ring he wore on his right hand. His voice was low as he continued. "It was a hard birth. The boy lived through it. She didn't. I gave her a golden ring to wear in her grave."

He emptied his glass in one swallow and set it on the table. "So now here I sit with a youngster I never wanted instead of her, the one I did want."

He refilled the glass. "He killed his mother, he did."

Eidi was about to protest, but a tone in her ear made her stop.

She said nothing but sat waiting, without knowing what it was she was waiting for. Then she looked across at Bandon, who had leaned back in his chair again.

"A baby can't help being born," she said at last.

He didn't answer.

After a moment he got up, went over to a table against the wall, and opened a little wooden chest that was on it. He took something out of it and brought it to her. He took her hand, put something in it, and then sat down again. "That's for you, if you promise me to keep it always."

A little golden arrow, mounted on a pin to make a brooch, shone on her palm.

"I promise," she said as she stood up. "Thank you."

"There's a candlestick over there on the table," he said, without turning his head. Eidi saw now that the candle she had brought from the kitchen had burned out some time ago.

"Thank you," she said again, and went quietly out the way she had come.

10

The sky hung low, as heavy and shaggy as the underbelly of an old dog. The wind whipped the screaming of the gulls far and wide. The fishing boats hugged the coast and caught next to nothing. All the petals had fallen from Lesna's roses. The thyme and sage had been cut and tied into bunches that hung on the rafters in the kitchen. Eidi shivered all night in her cold little room and longed to be off.

Rossan had finally bought a horse, a handsome, dark-brown animal with a light-brown mane and tail. Now the horse stood in the stable and whickered secrets in Lesna's horse's ear, secrets that only horses know.

When Eidi closed her eyes at night, she saw miles and miles of cloth with stripes and checks in every color wool can have.

And during the day she sat in the poorly lit room and strained her eyes at the loom. Tink came by every day, sat down hungrily at the table, and stuffed himself, so that Lesna complained about Eidi's great appetite.

Eidi had taught Tink to sew fringes on the shawls, and Bandon turned a blind eye and let them carry on, because the shawls sold well, and there were never enough of them in the shop.

"I'll be leaving soon."

Tink raised his head and stared at her. His gray-green eyes gleamed with mute terror. His jaws stopped chewing, and he sat there stock-still with his mouth full of food.

"Eat up," said Eidi, bending over the loom, and he gulped down the mouthful.

He said nothing, and neither did she, but shortly afterward there came a long-drawn-out sniff, and she glanced up at him.

"Oh, Tink!"

His nose was running freely, and his eyes were wet with tears. She reached out a hand to stroke his hair, but he jumped to his feet and plunged out of the room.

She didn't run after him, because she counted on him showing up again when he got hungry. But he didn't come the next day, or the day after. Not until a couple of days later did she hear his step in the short corridor that led to the weaving room.

He came in and sat at the table. Eidi put food in front of him: slices of cold beef, parsnips seasoned with herb vinegar, a piece of bread, and a couple of crisp small cakes filled with nuts and raisins.

"It's my birthday today," he told her.

"Is it? Many happy returns! Did you get lots of presents?"

Tink nodded and showed her a little knife that the old, bent-backed servant had laid beside his bed.

"And these here," he said, pulling a pair of knitted mittens out of his jacket pocket. "I got these from the cook. And the shop clerk gave me these."

He pulled a twist of paper containing raisins from his other pocket.

"What did you get from Bandon?" Eidi wanted to know.

"Nothing," answered Tink, and put the mittens and the packet of raisins back in his pockets. "He's always hated my birthday. He doesn't want me to have been born. He says it's my fault my mother died."

"He misses her."

"So do I," said Tink, sighing.

"I want you to have something from me, too," Eidi said hurriedly. "I'm going to weave you a neck scarf, and you can choose just how it should look."

His face lit up, and they were soon engrossed in looking over the different-colored wool and debating checks and stripes and length of fringes. Then Bandon suddenly appeared in the doorway.

"Didn't I tell you to take that crate down to the ship?" he bawled at Tink. "And there it still stands in the yard!"

"I tried, but I couldn't lift it."

"Damn it, that's because you sit skulking with the womenfolk all day!" Bandon lifted his hand and stepped toward Tink.

"You're not to hit him," said Eidi, getting to her feet.

Bandon turned and looked at her without lowering his hand. She looked directly into his pale face with the moist lips and the drops of sweat under the grizzled curls. His brown eyes looked almost black.

"And you're not to hit me either," she said sternly.

He let his hand fall, but the look in his eyes warned her not to dare interfere ever again. Then he grabbed Tink by the shoulder and dragged him out of the room and up into the yard.

Eidi watched as he shook the boy while he rained abuse on his head. She clenched her fists in fury, and the howling in her head nearly drove her mad.

At last she could stand it no longer. She flung herself across the room and out the door, only to see Bandon shove Tink down into the potato cellar at the side of the dog kennel. The watchdog broke into frenzied barking when Bandon let the trapdoor fall with a crash. Eidi retreated swiftly into the passage as he turned back to the main house.

Tink's desperate screams mingled with the wild barking of the dog. Eidi held her hands over her ears, and still heard it all.

For the rest of the day Tink sat in the dark cellar. Eidi didn't dare do anything, because Bandon was continually crossing the yard to the shop to fill his decanter, then going back again to the house.

Evening was falling, which made Eidi even more sorry for Tink, until she remembered that he had been sitting in the dark all day long.

She had been weaving his scarf the whole time, and even though in a way it was stealing from Bandon, to give his wool away without asking, that didn't worry her. After all, why shouldn't Bandon give Tink a birthday present, even though he didn't know he was doing it?

It was almost dark when Eidi saw the head clerk come down the steps of the shop with Bandon, who locked the door after them. The clerk left by the courtyard entryway, and Bandon went over to the main house with his replenished decanter.

Eidi wrapped the finished scarf around her neck, tiptoed to the yard door, and listened. The only sound she could hear was a cautious growl from the kennel.

"Nice doggy," she whispered. "Just look what I have for you!"

She tossed a thick slice of beef over to him, and

she could hear his tail thumping on the cobbles as he snatched up the meat. Then she walked right up to him and held out another piece, and the dog went on wagging his tail.

She scratched him behind the ears the way she had seen Tink do, and the dog let her and went on lying where he was.

Then she stole over to the cellar door and tried to open it, but it was much too heavy.

"Tink," she whispered, but no one answered.

"Tink!" she called a little louder.

Not a sound.

"Tink!" she shouted, loud and short, and a soft rustling and a subdued "Yes" told her that he had heard her.

"Push up on the trapdoor," she whispered, "and I'll get you out."

She heaved on the door herself for all she was worth, and on the other side she could hear Tink bracing his feet against the steps, and at last the trapdoor gave a little, only to fall back again.

"Once more, on the count of three," she whispered.

"I can't," groaned Tink.

"You've got to!"

Just as she said it, the watchdog began to bark. Only a few short barks, but enough that a window in the house opened and Bandon's voice bellowed into the night: "Shut up, dog!" The dog stopped barking, and the window was closed.

"Both together now," whispered Eidi. "One! Two! Three!" and the trapdoor came open and fell to the side with a crash.

Someone lit a candle in one of the windows. Eidi reached down into the darkness, grabbed Tink's hand, and pulled him toward her.

"Run!" she said urgently and dragged him out of the entryway and through the narrow streets as fast as she could go.

Only when they were right up by Lesna's house did they slacken their pace, and Eidi let Tink rest in a narrow alley close by while she crept up and peeped through the windows. Rossan and Lesna were sitting in the living room, just as usual.

Eidi fetched Tink and led him across the house yard, through her little room, and into the stable. There she took the scarf from her neck and draped it around his.

"Happy birthday," she said.

Then she pointed to a narrow ladder leaning under a trapdoor in a corner.

"Climb up into the loft and hide," she said. "And stay there no matter what happens. I'll bring you something to eat." Tink did as she said.

Alone, she sat on her settle bed for a minute to gather her wits. Then she stood up and went across to the living room.

11

When Eidi joined Rossan and Lesna, she tried her best to seem just as usual. She told them what she'd been doing all day, as she always did. In her tale she altered Tink's neck scarf to a shawl for the shop.

Then she asked Lesna if she could make herself a bite to eat before going to bed. Lesna looked at her, shaking her head.

"I don't think I ever met anybody who could eat like you. Where do you put it all? Because it doesn't show on you. Anyway, it's not good for you to eat just before bedtime."

Nevertheless Lesna got up, went to the kitchen, and brought back a platter with cold meat pie, a hard-boiled egg, a slice of thickly buttered bread, and three little pickles.

"Thanks very much. I'll just take it over to my room," said Eidi.

Rossan sent her a searching look but said nothing. Lesna sat back down with her knitting. "You do that. And sleep well," she said without glancing up. But Rossan's eyes followed Eidi all the way to the door.

As she shot the latch on the outer door of the room, a click sounded in her ear, and the little, shrill howl began. Eidi set the platter on the footstool by her bed and hurried into the stable.

Tink stuck his head out when he heard her coming.

"Hide yourself really well," whispered Eidi. "Crawl right down under the hay in the far corner."

Tink nodded and withdrew. She hurried back to her room and closed the inner door, shoving the footstool against it, as if she never went into the stable that way. She took off her clothes and laid them on the stool, shoved the platter under the bed, blew out the candle, and burrowed deep under the covers.

"Who else could it be?" bellowed a voice outside in the dark a moment later.

"He must have climbed out by himself," she heard Rossan argue.

"Impossible. The cellar door is much too heavy for that spindly brat. Somebody helped him, and it can only be her, because otherwise the watchdog would have barked the house down."

"Then it must have been one of the servants."

"Impossible," snapped Bandon.

Rossan came into the room with Bandon on his heels. He set the lantern on the floor by the door and came over to the bed.

"Eidi," he called.

She sat up, rubbing her eyes.

"Do you know where Tink is?" he asked her kindly.

"He's shut in," Eidi answered without hesitation. She rolled over on her side and pretended to go back to sleep.

"Where does that door lead?"

Bandon was pointing with his stick at the door behind the stool.

"Into the stable. But that's enough now," said

Rossan. "This is no way to behave, disturbing folks'
rest. And what can you be thinking of, shutting a
child up—"

Bandon kicked the stool aside and opened the
door to the stable. Then he picked up the lantern
and went in. Rossan followed him. Eidi lay quite
still with the covers pulled over her ears. She could
hear mice rummaging around the platter under the
bed, but she couldn't risk chasing them away.

There was a sound like a branch snapping.

"That confounded boy! When I catch him I'll
wring his neck!"

"That ladder won't bear your weight," came
Rossan's calm voice. "You'd better let me look."

Eidi held her breath and listened in the darkness
of her room. Some time passed.

"Not even a cat up here," Rossan called, short of
breath. And a little later, when he had come down
by the ladder: "Now it's high time we had some
peace and quiet for the night."

Bandon searched the stable, poking into the hay
with his stick, but at last he let himself be escorted
out the door. Shortly afterward Eidi heard Bandon
stumbling and cursing in the alley leading out to

the street, then Rossan's voice: "Yes, it's not easy finding your way in the dark. Let me light you home."

Eidi stayed where she was until the sound of footsteps had ceased. Then she got up. She called Tink, who hurried down to her. He was trembling all over.

"Hurry up and take off your trousers!" she commanded.

"But—"

"Nobody must recognize you. You're going to wear my skirt. We're going to dress you as a girl and me as a boy."

Tink did as she said. She helped him into the skirt and found a piece of rope in the stable to hold it up around his waist. She pulled his jacket down so the rope couldn't be seen and wound his new scarf around his head so no one could see his short hair.

She herself put on Kotka's work trousers, which were hanging on a nail in the stable. She put on his old sweater to cover the rest.

"You still look like a girl," said Tink.

Eidi grabbed her long, thick braid and stuffed it down the neck of the sweater. She took the blanket off the bed and made a bundle of the rest of their clothes. She remembered to take her scissors and some other useful things as well.

Then she thought of the platter under the bed, but when she pulled it out, only the three little pickles were left. They would have to start off without provisions.

She put out the candle and stood listening with the stable door open a crack until she heard Rossan come back and close the front house door after him. Then she took Tink's clammy little hand in one of hers, and the halter in the other, and led both him and Rossan's horse out of the stable, down the alley, and onto the road.

The sound of the horse's hooves rang out in the quiet of the night, but there was a seaward wind that carried the clatter out over the bay, away from the house and Lesna's ears. The sky was heavy with rain clouds, and now and then a drop splashed on their faces.

In order to get clear of the town, they had to cross the marketplace. And in order to find the path over the hills, they had to pass by Bandon's house. Light was streaming from the windows of the big room, and Eidi hesitated, uncertain what to do.

"Let's take the coast road," Tink suggested. "I know the way. There's a town at the other end of it."

From Bandon's house, they could hear voices and a barking dog, and Eidi wasn't certain that she could find the hill path in the dark, so she decided to follow Tink's advice. They would have to turn inland farther up the coast.

They led the horse cautiously along the quay, and when they were well outside of town, they got on his back and rode into the dark.

12

The sun rose over the sea, and its light found a way through clouds and fogbanks to shine on the two children on horseback. It touched them with a hint of warmth and the promise of more.

Eidi was beginning to realize what she had done. She had stolen a blanket from Lesna, and Rossan's horse as well. She had left her place with Rossan, quit her job, and kidnapped Bandon's child. Or rather his deceased betrothed's child, or whatever one could call this skinny small boy whose hands were holding on to her waist.

"I can see where your braid starts," Tink observed.

"We'll stop for a rest in a little while. I'll attend to it then. Keep an eye out for a stream, so we can wash our faces and get a drink."

Before long they found a place. A little brook ran under a bridge that was part of the road. The rippling water was clear and cold, and it soothed their empty stomachs. The horse turned his attention to the withered yellow grass.

Eidi sat down and dug out her scissors. She handed them to Tink. "Cut off my braid as close to my head as you can," she told him.

The scissors were new and sharp. Even so, it took Tink quite a while to cut the hair off. When he was through, he handed her the braid. She wrapped it in her knitted head scarf and put it in the bundle.

Then she cut the rest of her hair herself. She lifted lock after lock from her scalp between two fingers and cut off the ends, so at last her hair was the same length all over.

"You're getting curls!" said Tink, laughing.

Eidi felt her head. Yes, it was true. Her hair, which had been pulled smooth by its length and weight, had now gone all frisky with its lightness and was curling merrily all by itself.

"You look completely different. You don't seem like yourself at all."

She looked at him.

"You should see yourself, then," Eidi said.

He really did look like a little girl. The long knitted scarf hid his hair, except for what fell down across his forehead. Beneath this light-brown fringe a pair of gray-green eyes smiled at her. His shabby, skimpy jacket hugged his figure down to the waist, and under that the skirt widened out. It reached right to the ground, so that only the toes of a pair of brown boots peeped out.

"What's your name, if anyone should ask?"

Tink thought it over. "Askja," he suggested.

Eidi nodded. "And I'm called Eski. We are on our way to our granny, our mother's mother, because our mother is sick. A fox ate our food while we were sleeping, and . . ."

". . . now we need some bread and cheese and sausage," said Tink, laughing. Then he was suddenly serious. "We really do, don't we?"

"But our dear mother gave us a little purse of money to take along," Eidi continued, shaking the leather pouch that hung at her belt, so that the coins chinked together, "so we can buy what we need . . ."

". . . if there was any place to buy it," said Tink, sighing.

"We'll find somewhere," she assured him, getting to her feet.

At that moment she caught sight of two riders on their way toward them from the seaport town.

"Look there!" shouted Tink. His voice shook a little.

Eidi listened for the howl inside her ear, but she heard only outer sounds—the gurgle of water between stones, the cry of a gull, the pounding of hooves coming closer and closer.

Tink took her hand, and she gave his a little squeeze.

"Askja," she said. "Remember, now."

He nodded.

The two riders came right up to them and stopped. Eidi looked up. The one was a woman and the other— It was her stepfather.

"Good day to you, children," he said, without looking closely at them. He got off the horse and went to fill his water jug from the brook.

Eidi noticed a big haversack hanging at the side of the woman's horse. She went over to her.

"We've lost our provisions. Could we buy a little food from you? I have some money," she said warily, taking a few coins out of her pouch.

"Well, I don't know about that," said the woman, meeting Eidi's and Tink's longing gazes.

"Burd!" she called.

The man came toward them.

"Can't we sell the children some of our provisions? They've lost theirs."

Eidi's stepfather was close by now and looked down at them.

"What are you called?"

"Eski," answered Eidi.

"And my name is Askja," Tink said. "We're on our way to our granny, because our mother is sick."

"That's a pity," said Burd. "And now you have no food. Jona, let them have the cooked sausage and a loaf of bread, and the little brown cheese."

The woman found the food in the haversack and handed it to the children. Eidi held some coins out to Burd.

"No, no. I wouldn't hear of it." He refused the

money with a shake of the head. "A body can always spare a bit of food. As long as you're not after my brandy," he said, laughing. Suddenly he stopped laughing. It was as if he saw Eidi for the first time, and he searched her face intently.

"See here, haven't we met before?" he asked.

"Maybe," she answered. "I was at the market."

"Oh, then it must have been there I saw you. There isn't a market anywhere that I haven't been at. We're on our way to another one now."

"Well, we wouldn't want to delay you," Eidi said eagerly. "And thanks for the food."

She managed to remember just in time not to bob a curtsy. He patted her cheek.

"Your mother must be proud to have a handsome boy like you," he said kindly, and mounted his horse.

"Off we go!" he shouted, and he and the woman rode on.

Now they had Burd ahead of them and Bandon behind. And Eidi didn't care to meet either of them again.

She broke off some bread for herself and Tink, and as they ate she told Tink who Burd was.

"Why, he seemed really kind," said Tink, puzzled.

"He is, when he's sober," answered Eidi. "But now he's on his way to a market, and then he'll get drunk, and then I'd hate to have him get the notion that he knows me."

They walked down the road leading the horse. Eidi didn't want to risk catching up with Burd, but at the same time she was nagged by the fear that Bandon might catch up with them.

Then she caught sight of a narrow track winding inland off the road. And even if it might not be anything more than an animal trail, she decided to follow it.

"This way," she told Tink.

They got on the horse and rode up the track, away from the highway and the sea.

The sun warmed their backs despite the cold wind. Orange lichen glowed on the gray stones. A bird of prey circled overhead, and Eidi drew a deep breath. Then she began to sing, louder and louder, till it felt as though she was drawing the pearly sky closer to them.

❧

They had been riding for a long time when Eidi felt Tink's grip slacken on her waist.

"Hey, I think you're falling asleep," she said to him.

"Yes, I guess I am," he mumbled.

So they stopped and found a sun-warmed hollow, curled up like two tired animals under the blanket, and fell asleep.

13

When Eidi woke, the sun was low in the sky. Tink was still asleep at her side, and it was tempting to stay under the blanket until the next morning. But if they got up now, they could ride for a couple of hours before dark. Eidi didn't feel they had gotten far enough from the town yet. She woke Tink, and when they had each eaten a slice of bread with some sausage, they continued their journey.

They had been riding over bare bedrock, where only a bit of lichen grew, but now the landscape was changing. They passed the outer tip of the stony ridge that Eidi and Rossan had crossed on their way to the seaport town, and now they came to the heath, where the heather had clothed the countryside in a furry brown winter coat. Willow scrub and dwarf oak trees stuck up here and there. And now and then a boghole showed a yellow warning.

It was easier to follow the track here than across the bare rock. It wound carefully in and out around trees and bogholes, but Eidi wouldn't have liked to travel along it after dark.

"We'll have to look out for somewhere to spend the night," she said.

"Mmmm," mumbled Tink.

He would have been happy to stay asleep in the hollow, and if it hadn't been for Eidi's singing, he would have fallen asleep behind her on the horse.

Then, in the distance, Eidi caught sight of a little light-gray block in the midst of the dark heather. It was a stone house with a single chimney, but there was no smoke curling up from it. A low stable stood close by. There were no animals or people in sight.

"That's strange," said Eidi, when they had ridden right up to the place. "Nobody seems to live here, but still the house doesn't have an abandoned look."

They got down off the horse, and Eidi went over and knocked on the door. There was no answer, so she tried the latch—the door wasn't locked—and went in.

There was just one room, with a fireplace, two settle beds, a table, and a chair. The walls were whitewashed and hung with deerskins. The stone floor was swept clean, with only a fine film of dust to show that it was some time since anyone had been there.

What sort of place is this? wondered Eidi.

There was a candlestick on the table. She lit the candle in it using the tinderbox that she found on the mantel. A fire had been laid ready for lighting. A basket by the fireplace was full of dry firewood.

"Don't you think we should light the fire?" Tink suggested, shivering in the evening chill.

"Get the blanket and wrap yourself up," she told him. "First I have to find out what sort of house this is."

"It's probably just a hunting lodge," Tink suggested.

"A hunting lodge!" exclaimed Eidi. She had never heard of such a thing.

"Yes, a hunting lodge," insisted Tink, "like the one Bandon has. Every so often he goes off to it with Ram—"

"Ram?"

"Yes. You know! The old servant. And the dog, and they hunt deer and game fowl. It stands all by itself on the heath beyond the Gray Mountains—"

"Gray Mountains?"

"Yes, the ridge of hills behind the town. I've never been there. Ram is the only one he lets go with him. Bandon always calls it 'his own place,' and—"

"And this is it!" exclaimed Eidi in alarm, and dashed out of the house.

Outside she stood still, listening in the dusk: the cry of a bird, the whisper of a dry tuft of grass, someone breathing . . .

She spun around and saw that Tink had crept out of the house after her and was standing close behind her.

"Hadn't we better get out of here?" he asked, torn between travel weariness and fear.

Eidi shook her head.

"No one will be coming here now," she said.

"Listen. There's not a sound, and in a little while it will be so dark that it would be too dangerous to ride out here, with all those bogholes, even for someone who knew the way. We'll stay here tonight, and be on our way as soon as it's light."

But she didn't feel very safe as they lay under the blanket. Tink fell asleep right away, clutching her hand. But she pried it free and clasped her hands under her head. She lay that way a long time, staring up into the darkness.

She must have slept. Her arms and legs were heavy, like stones, and she couldn't move them. Then the dream stole gradually into her memory:

Bandon, who kept insisting, "I have something to tell you," and she, who didn't want to hear it, and could keep from hearing it only by waking herself.

But even now it was as if Bandon were there in the room.

She sat up in alarm and looked around her in the pale dawn light that was seeping in from outside. Tink had curled himself into a ball, as he usually did when he slept. Except for them, the room was empty.

She woke him, and after tidying the house they went on their way without eating. Not even the burned-out candle could show they had been there, because Eidi had found a whole bundle of candles in the drawer of the table and put a fresh one in the candlestick.

They didn't stop until they came to a ford. Tink went behind a bush to pee. It always took him a terribly long time, because he had difficulties with the skirt.

Eidi sat down with her back against a stone. She unbuttoned the neck of Kotka's old sweater and took off the gold arrow brooch that she had fastened inside it. She was just about to throw it into the water when her ear clicked. Before the howling tone could start, she had pinned it back on again.

I'll wait, she thought. I'm sure I can rid myself of it one way or another. She didn't want to have anything to do with something that had belonged to Bandon.

Later that day she tried again to get rid of the little gold brooch. As they rode she unclasped it from the inside of the sweater and let it fall on the path. And, so as not to be distracted by clicks and howls, she sang a loud song about working on the loom, about weaving rag rugs: how the dreary warp, the up-and-down threads, the daily drudgery, are there to hold fast the side-to-side weft, the thin strips of many-hued fabrics, all the color and festivity of life.

But the next time they stopped to rest, Tink said, "Look what's dangling there."

And there was the golden arrow hanging from the blanket that wrapped their bundle. The pin had stuck in the cloth as it fell, and there it had hung all that way.

Eidi sighed, took the brooch, and pinned it back inside Kotka's old sweater.

When it was getting dark, they stopped for the night in a little dell with grassy sides. And that night Eidi dreamed again of Bandon. They were sitting by the fire and gazing at the colors of the flames. Bandon was younger and handsomer. His curls were all brown, and his mouth was red-lipped and generous. "Shall I tell you a story?" he asked in a friendly tone. And she was just about to say yes when she realized that it was a trap, that he was going to make her hear what she didn't want to know.

So she woke herself up and lay for a long time listening to the cold wind soughing over the heath. It could not reach them down in the little dell.

14

The day after, they came to the high road that ran from north to south. Eidi had not yet decided if she wanted to ride to Crow Cove first and then ride over to Rossan's with the horse—because of course he had to have his horse back—or if it was better to take the horse to Rossan's first and then walk the long way home to Crow Cove with Tink.

It was the sausage and bread and cheese that made up her mind for her. They had eaten every last bit of it, and hunger was gripping Eidi's insides.

And she was worried about Tink. His little head was dangling wearily on his long, slender neck. But it couldn't be sickness, because he was fiercely hungry. It was as if he had been holding a deathly tiredness at bay for a long time, and now it had caught up with him and wouldn't let him go. And he had no strength left to fight it off. At last she took the skirt off him, got him into pants, and used the rope that had held the skirt up to tie him to her back so that he wouldn't tumble off the horse if he should fall asleep.

It was late afternoon when they came to the bend in the road and she saw Rossan's house.

"Tink," she called.

He mumbled something behind her.

"Look! There's the house!"

The dogs began to bark as they drew near, and Kotka appeared in the doorway.

"Hey there! Who are you?" he called.

"It's me!" shouted Eidi in reply.

Then she suddenly remembered her short hair. "It's Eidi. I cut my hair."

She untied the rope from around herself and Tink, got off the horse, and went up to Kotka.

"I wouldn't have known you at all," he said, staring. "You look like a boy, and— Hey, that's my sweater you're wearing—and my trousers."

"I'll tell you all about it," she said, "but first I want you to say hello to Tink."

She turned around and saw that he had fallen asleep sitting up on the horse's back. The scarf had slid off his head and hung in its proper place around his neck. Then he started to droop to one side, toward them. Kotka caught him just before he fell off the horse.

They carried him inside and laid him in the settle bed. And then Eidi sat down at the table and told the whole story, while Kotka heated up some broth.

When she had finished and was sitting with the big, steaming bowl in front of her, she asked anxiously, "You won't tell Lesna, will you?"

"I wouldn't dream of it," Kotka assured her. "There's already quite a lot she doesn't know about. It's not good for some people to know too much. And she'd let on to that old skirt chaser right away, and he'd come running out here. And we don't want that."

At last Eidi could breathe freely. She began on the broth and burned her mouth so that her tongue felt thick. But she kept eating until the bowl was empty and her stomach was filled.

Tink slept for a whole day and a whole night. Then he woke up and ate an enormous helping of broth and fell asleep again.

He lay quite still, with unmoving eyelids, and you couldn't see his breathing. He was pale, but when Eidi put her hand to his face or his arm, it felt right, so he didn't have a fever.

Sometimes she pulled her chair up to the settle bed and sang to him—the song about weaving the rag rug—because she thought it must be lonesome to be away from life for so long.

But when Tink finally woke up, it turned out that he hadn't been lonely at all. He had dreamed that he was so happy he sang as he walked along a road that wound between green hills. Then suddenly it occurred to him that he had no business being happy, since it was his fault his mother was dead.

But then he met his mother. She looked like Eidi, and came right toward him. She was singing as she walked, too, and when she reached him, she bent down and kissed him. She went singing on her way, and from far down the road she turned and waved to him. And then he woke up.

All the weariness seemed to have been washed

out of him. His eyes shone green and clear as he looked around with pleasure. He went out with Kotka to the sheep and returned delighted.

"You should have seen the dog," he told Eidi. "She can gather all the sheep together in a minute. She runs behind them and darts from one side to the other so they can't slip away."

Eidi nodded absentmindedly while she went on carding the tuft of wool she had on the combs. She had been working constantly since they arrived, while she waited for Tink to be ready to continue their journey.

All the wool Rossan had not sold at the market, because she was to have spun it during the winter, was lying in big bales in the attic, spreading the odor of sheep through the house. But now that winter was almost gone and Tink was able to continue their journey, Eidi was in no hurry to leave—she wanted to attend to that wool.

And yet she felt uneasy. She was afraid that they would be discovered, and that Tink would be forced to return to Bandon.

"You can hide in the attic if anyone comes," Kotka suggested. He didn't want them to leave either.

"But what about the horse?" asked Eidi.

"I'll just say it's mine," said Kotka.

So they stayed on.

Eidi worked out her unrest through her hands. Skeins of gray, brown, black, and creamy white yarn began to pile up in place of the bales. She taught Tink to card wool. Day after day he sat, his long, white neck bent over the carding combs, until suddenly one day Eidi saw him as a featherless fledgling, perched on a twig with a drooping beak. So she sent him off with Kotka and the young sheepdog. Old Glennie stayed in the house with her.

Kotka took care of everything else, so that Eidi could give all her attention to the wool. He looked after the sheep, fed the horse and the dogs, made soup and broth and stews of mutton and potatoes, swept, washed clothes, and scrubbed Tink from top to toe.

Eidi began to feel safe. It was a long while since she had dreamed of Bandon, and Burd was far away—even in her thoughts.

Then suddenly one day Kotka rushed into the room with Tink at his heels. "Hurry!" he said urgently. "Get up in the attic! There's someone riding along the path from town."

Eidi dropped everything, and she and Tink scrambled up the steps into the murky attic and hid in the farthest corner. She could hear Kotka bumping around downstairs, hastily hiding anything that might betray them.

Then suddenly she heard a familiar voice at the foot of the stairs. "My, my. What a flurry you're in," said Rossan.

15

Eidi held back a bit at first, but all she saw on Rossan's weathered face was a wide smile. She threw herself into his arms.

"I stole your horse," she mumbled into his sweater.

"No you didn't," he said, giving her a quick hug. "You just rode it home for me. There it is, out in the stable, isn't it?"

"I took a blanket from Lesna."

"Well yes, that was worse. She's so fussy about her things. But you only borrowed it without asking leave, and Kotka can take it back to her.

"So this is the rascal who caused all that commotion."

Tink had come down from the attic. He stood at the foot of the steep stairs looking rather forlorn. Rossan went over and shook hands with him. Both the dogs followed close beside him, wagging their tails. Rossan sat down on the bench, scratched them behind the ears, and patted their heads. Then he looked up at Eidi.

"We have such a lot to talk about that I don't know where to begin. But first let's have a bite to eat. Kotka, your mother must think we don't have a scrap of food in the house. Just open that bag and see what she sent with me!"

And Kotka pulled meat pies, salt pickles, sausages, cheese, hard-boiled eggs, baked potatoes and parsnips, and bread and butter out of the bag.

While they ate, Rossan told how Bandon had searched for them for several days but had finally given up, declaring that since, after all, Tink was no son of his, he could go where he pleased and much good might it do him.

Tink had been sitting very still, slowly peeling an egg. Now the anxious look disappeared from his face, and his appetite returned. He attacked the provisions and ate hungrily.

Eidi knew that Rossan had more to tell her, but she didn't ask. She would wait until Tink had gone to bed. Kotka must have felt the same, because he started talking about the sheep and the dogs, and Rossan inquired about the wool, and Eidi proudly showed him the skeins of yarn.

Darkness fell, and Tink began to yawn. "Come along, I'll tuck you in upstairs," said Eidi.

"But Rossan has so much to tell," protested Tink.

"You've heard the most important news," said Rossan, "and that's that you can sleep easy now. You'll hear the rest as we go along."

So Tink gave in—he was very tired—and went with Eidi up to the attic. He was asleep before Eidi had sung one verse of a song.

The house seemed to have taken on new life now that Rossan was back. It felt warmer and cozier, and only now that he was here did Eidi realize how much she had missed him.

The flames from the hearth set the shadows dancing on the whitewashed walls, and the good smell of food mingled with the homely smell of raw wool. An occasional thump of a dog's tail on the floor told that one of them had suddenly remembered all over again that Rossan had come home. And an occasional little hop of joy in Eidi's chest said the same.

At the same time, she realized that it wasn't just Rossan himself she had missed. She had also missed having a grownup. Even though Kotka was big and strong, he was still only a boy, and what could a boy do against Burd and Bandon?

She had taken out the carding combs and was sitting by the fire. At the back of the room, Kotka was clattering with the dishes.

"That night Bandon came, did you know I'd hidden him?" asked Eidi.

Rossan nodded. "At first I just had a suspicion, but when I looked up in the hayloft, I knew for certain."

"Did you see him?" asked Eidi in surprise.

"To be sure I did. He had hidden his head and most of his body, but his little behind was sticking up in the air." said Rossan, laughing. "But I told the truth. I said there wasn't a cat up there, and there wasn't."

Eidi joined his laughter. "I told the truth, too. I

said he was shut in, and so he was—up in the loft."

"Yes indeed, it's not good to have to tell lies," said Rossan, "but it's good to be able to, even if you have to tell the truth to do it.

"The next day I didn't let on. I complained about you stealing the horse, and that if you showed up at my place I'd give you what for. And I spun a long yarn about how you'd never dream of going back to Crow Cove, because you had fallen out with your mother and Frid."

"But I haven't."

"I had to say something to stop them from looking for you there."

He filled his pipe and lit it, and the spicy fragrance of tobacco mingled with the room's other odors.

"He's right—Bandon. There are lots of colors in the fire." Eidi looked at Rossan in amazement. He went on, "You see, I could have spared myself all my yarns, but I didn't know that until I'd talked with him."

Eidi laid the carding combs aside. Kotka joined them by the fire.

"At first he searched all over town. Then it occurred to him that Tink might have remembered about his hunting lodge. So he went out there. But there didn't seem to have been anyone in it, so he decided to spend the night there and ride on in the morning. He lit a fire and sat and watched the flames. He told me he sat there thinking of you." Rossan looked up at Eidi. "That was when he said that about all the colors there are in the fire."

Eidi nodded.

"He said that as he sat there, he realized he had tormented both himself and the boy by keeping him in his household—that he should have found a good family for the boy long ago."

"Then why didn't he?" said Eidi angrily.

Rossan shrugged.

"He just wanted somebody to take it all out on," Eidi fumed.

Rossan's pipe had gone out. He lit it again. "Maybe he was lonely. Maybe he thought he owed it to the boy's mother to provide for him. I don't know. Everyone has to be allowed to grow some wisdom—"

"And shake the stone out of his shoe," Eidi suggested.

Rossan nodded and took a puff of his pipe. A greenish flame sprang out of the log at the back of the fireplace, and Eidi could feel something hard and tight inside her soften and unfold.

"He told me that when he discovered you had been in the lodge after all, he realized that it wasn't Tink he had been looking for. It was you."

"How could he have known I'd been there?"

"You'd put a new candle in the candlestick, evidently a different kind than the ones he ordinarily uses, one from a fresh bundle in the drawer. He sat up all night, and as soon as it was light, he saddled his horse and rode back to the town. Then he came calling on me."

Rossan stood up. "I have something for you."

He fetched a pouch and handed it to her. Eidi opened it and stared at all the golden coins in it.

"Bandon says that what's left when you've taken the rest of your wages is to be spent to provide for Tink, and for you as long as you look after him."

"But . . . how could he know you would find me here?"

"He didn't," said Rossan. "But I told him that sooner or later I was pretty sure to see you again."

Then he brought a bundle packed in a worn silk kerchief. "These are the things Bandon bought from Tink's mother when she came sailing to the town."

Eidi opened the bundle carefully. The kerchief had almost moldered away in several places. Inside were a worn silver hair clasp, a yellowed comb made of bone, a child's thimble, a small ring set with a green stone, a finely turned wooden case containing a couple of rusted needles, and ten little mother-of-pearl buttons, shimmering with green, white, silver, and blue—even more beautiful than the ones Eidi had lost.

"He wanted you to keep these things and give them to Tink some time or other."

"I will, for sure," said Eidi. She packed them carefully back into the kerchief.

16

The rain blew in from the sea and slashed against the windows. They had to have candles lit all day long. The fire blazed on the hearth and kept the stew bubbling in the pot, so the good smell of cooking was always in the room.

Kotka and Tink were out with the sheep. Eidi sat spinning, filling the room with the soothing hum of the wheel. Old Glennie lay asleep in her place by the door, thumping the floor with her tail now and then when she had good dreams. The clicks of Rossan's knitting needles mingled with the other sounds.

"If you'd like to knit yourself a sweater, just help yourself to yarn," he said.

"Thank you. Yes," said Eidi. "I'd like that."

She stopped the spinning wheel and flexed her fingers. She had been spinning yarn for days now and wanted to use her hands for something else.

"Yes, it's time for a change. It's not good to do one thing for too long at a time," observed Rossan.

He laid his knitting on the table and went over to stir the stew.

"We can eat as soon as the boys get in."

Old Glennie woke at the sound of his voice, got to her feet, and shuffled over to him. Eidi went up to the attic and surveyed the skeins of spun yarn. She was looking for something left over from a shawl that Rossan had knitted for Lesna.

But when she found the little light-gray ball, she could see that there wasn't enough for a sweater for herself. All the same, she couldn't give up the idea. The yarn was so soft and fine, and it was the same pearly gray color as an overcast sky.

I'll knit a tiny jacket, she thought, and took the yarn downstairs.

She began to cast on, but the yarn was so delicate

and fine that it broke when she tightened the stitches. So she went back up into the attic and fetched down her own long braid, which was still wound up in her knitted head scarf.

She started again on the jacket, but now she knitted her own long hairs gradually into the rows one by one, to strengthen the yarn. Whenever she got to the end of a hair, she pulled a new one from the thick, golden-red plait.

"That will make a warm, well-wearing jacket," remarked Rossan. "He'll be glad of that."

"Who will?"

"Your little brother, to be sure. Cam—isn't that his name? He's the only one that size I know of."

And of course that was so.

At last one day it stopped raining. Kotka wanted to ride to town and see Lesna, and then he intended to come back in time to look after the sheep while Rossan made his trip to the big spring market.

Rossan packed provisions for him and gave him a shawl to take to Lesna that he had knitted for her. Eidi asked him to give Lesna one of her golden coins to pay for her board and lodging, not to forget to return the blanket, and to tell her thanks for the loan of it.

"Isn't there something you'd like me to bring you from town?" Kotka asked Eidi.

She hesitated.

"You name it! I'll be back sooner or later, you know. And if you've left by the time I get back, I'll ride out to Crow Cove. I've always wanted to have a look at that place."

"Well, if you could buy five mother-of-pearl buttons for the little jacket. No, just four, because I have one already. You can take it with you so you can get them to match."

She ran up to the attic and brought it down to him. He put it in his jacket pocket and pulled his knitted cap down over his white, unruly hair.

"And—" she began, and then stopped.

"Yes?"

"A horse."

"A horse?"

"Yes. Tink and I have such a lot of money, so I thought maybe we should buy a horse. Then we'd have something to ride to Crow Cove on. And we need a horse at home, too. The one Doup has is only big enough to carry him."

"Yes! Let's buy a horse!" Tink shouted happily.

Rossan thought it was a good idea, too. "Mind you, take your mother along when you buy it," he told Kotka. "Nobody can pull the wool over her eyes."

Kotka promised. Eidi gave him the money, and he started off.

One sunny day Eidi spun the last skein of wool. She rose from the spinning wheel, put it back into its corner, and went to wash the wool oil off her fingers. She would be paid for her work after Rossan had sold the yarn.

Then she sat down at the table and looked at the tiny jacket. It was finished now and lacked nothing but the five buttons. There was only a very small ball of yarn left, and with this she crocheted scallops around all the edges. Then she sewed in the yarn ends and folded it away.

The door stood open out to the farmyard. The low afternoon sun slanted in to her. She got up and went outside.

The air was crisp and clear and full of the wing-beats and voices of birds of passage coming home. Far away the sea lay sparkling blue in the sunlight. Feathery clouds floated across the sky.

Eidi drew a deep breath, stretched her arms over her head, and spread her fingers wide. A tingling ran all through her body. She felt so light, now that all the wool lay in neat skeins of yarn up in the attic. She had done the work she set out to do. Now she could do whatever she liked.

She went out behind the house and along the track that led toward Eastern Harbor. She picked some of the first downy pussy willows growing there. Then she heard a new sound, and far off she saw Kotka come riding along the track.

His flaxen-white hair shone in the sunlight, and she saw him lift his arm to wave as soon as he caught sight of her. He was riding Lesna's horse and leading a roan mare with a glossy black mane and tail.

The dogs had heard them and came running, leaping, and wagging all over. When they got to the house, Rossan was standing in the doorway, and Tink stuck his head out of the stable. When he saw the horse, he rushed into the yard.

"Is that one ours?" he shouted happily, running to catch hold of the bridle.

Kotka had brought much more. First he handed down the big haversack, which he put into Rossan's hands with many greetings from Lesna. He was to remember to say that she liked the shawl very much. He had a silver coin for Eidi from Lesna, because the gold coin was more than she was owed, his mother had said.

For Rossan he had bought tea and tobacco, as he had been asked to do, and a lot of different seeds that Rossan wanted Foula to have.

For Eidi, Kotka had bought *five* mother-of-pearl buttons, because he couldn't find any others that matched the one she had sent with him. He fished all six buttons out of his jacket pocket and handed them to her. The new ones he had found glimmered in soft shades of gray. At first Eidi was disappointed, but when she tried them against the jacket, she found that they suited it perfectly.

For Tink there was a paper twist full of raisins from Bandon's shop. Before Kotka had left, they had all agreed that it need not be a secret any longer that Eidi and Tink were staying with Rossan. Kotka had told no one but his mother. But Bandon was sure to know by now, because he and Lesna had begun to keep company pretty regularly.

"But now he'll come after us," Tink gasped,

dropping a raisin that he was about to put in his mouth.

Eidi picked up the raisin. "No, he won't," she said, and handed it back to him.

But that night she dreamed about Bandon for the first time in a long while:

She was sitting on the big, flat rock off the shore by Crow Cove when he rose up out of the sea in front of her. He was wearing his fur-trimmed winter coat. It was quite dry.

He came toward her, holding out a big mussel shell full of mother-of-pearl buttons. She felt a sudden fear that he was trying to fool her in some way.

Her fear woke her, and she found herself again in bed in Rossan's attic. She lay listening to Tink's easy breathing, with a strange feeling that she had been fooling herself.

17

Eidi helped Tink down off the mare. She had decided they should stop and rest at the big gray stone that loomed by the side of the road, marking the turnoff of the track down to Crow Cove. They leaned their backs against the sun-warmed stone and unpacked their provisions.

"What if your mother doesn't want me to live there?" mumbled Tink with his mouth full of smoked lamb.

"She will," said Eidi, and cut another slice of bread for them both.

They ate on in silence.

"What if Bandon finds us?" asked Tink while

Eidi was packing the provisions back in the haversack.

"He won't," she said. "Let's be on our way now." She didn't want to talk about Bandon.

"How do you know?" Tink said angrily. "You don't really know him at all. You don't know him the way I do."

She turned around and looked at him.

"Why shouldn't he find us there?" he went on, exasperated. "Kotka told his mother, and she told Bandon, and sooner or later he's going to come and take me back."

Eidi bent down and dug the little bundle out of their baggage. "I'll show you why he's never going to come after you again. Look what he sent you."

They sat down again against the stone.

"What is it?" he asked, his curiosity roused.

"Your mother came in a ship to the market, before you were born." He nodded. He knew that. "She sold everything she had, and Bandon bought it all. He has kept it ever since. He gave it to Rossan, who gave it to me, so that I could pass it on to you. I had thought I'd wait and give it to you when we got to Crow Cove, but you'd better have it now. Anyway, you must see that Bandon wouldn't send you a keepsake if he intended to chase after you and fetch you back."

Tink stared at the bundle but didn't touch it.

"Do you want me to unpack it?" she asked.

He nodded. Very gently she undid the folds of the fragile silk and showed him the silver hair clasp, the bone comb, the thimble and the ring, the needle case, and the ten mother-of-pearl buttons.

Tink picked up the things one after another and looked at them. At last he picked up the buttons and spread them out on his palm. Then he closed his hand on them and held it out to Eidi.

"Here. I want you to have these."

She shook her head. "No, they're yours."

"Yes, they are, so I can do what I like with them. Here!"

He held out his closed hand once more, and again she shook her head.

"Why can't I give you a gift?" His voice was shrill and his eyes were moist.

She reached out her hand and took them. "Thank you very much," she said, and put them in her pouch.

❧

The brook spread a silver-gray fan over the stony seashore. The three houses shone like little white building blocks against the gray-green grass. High over their heads, a hovering eagle greeted them with a scream.

"That's Crow Cove," said Eidi.

Tink stood silent for a moment; then he said, "I would like to live here."

They began the descent from the ridge. The path was narrow and steep, and they had to lead the mare. Eidi could feel her legs shaking a little. They had been traveling for many hours since they had rested by the big rock. Their feet were wet and cold from walking on the damp earth in the hollows.

The sun was low on the horizon and shone right in their faces, so it was hard to see where they were going. Tink stumbled, and Eidi caught him. When they had gotten down the steepest part, she helped him up on the horse again.

She was walking very slowly in order to relish every minute. There was the brook gurgling on its way, there was the big, flat rock, and there were the brown hens clucking about their own affairs. There was Myna's house, and there was her own, on the other side of the brook. There was a woven basket standing on the bench in the shadow of the eaves, and there was Foula working in the kitchen garden.

Eidi quickened her pace. Then she heard a shout from across the cove.

"Here come two boys!"

It was Ravnar who had caught sight of them. Foula straightened up and wiped her hands on her apron. Then she came down to the bridge. Eidi let go of the mare, who went to the brook to drink with Tink still on her back.

Eidi and Foula stood on each side of the bridge. For a moment Foula was looking at a tall boy in a pair of work-worn trousers, with longish, curly hair. Then she saw it was Eidi.

They met in the middle of the bridge, and Eidi let herself be engulfed by a pair of strong arms and a soft bosom. Then Foula took a step back, held her at arms' length, and took a good look at her.

"Can this really be you?" she asked her daughter.

Her eyes shone on Eidi. Then she embraced her again.

"And who's that boy? And whose is the horse?"

"That's Tink. He doesn't have any father or mother. He would like to live here, if you'll let him.

And the horse is ours, and I have some gifts for you from Rossan."

Then she took Foula's hand, and they crossed the bridge together and went over to the mare. Eidi helped Tink down. He stood there stiffly with his eyes on the ground. But Foula squatted in front of him and looked into the shy gray-green eyes.

"Hello," she said. "I'm Eidi's mother. Welcome to Crow Cove."

Then she took his hand. "Come along with me, and I'll show you where we live."

And Tink went along with her.

Many things had changed. Frid had built a room for Eidi while she was away. The door to it was beside the stairs. The bed was in a sort of alcove with a sloping ceiling. This ceiling was the underside of the stairs, boarded over with planks. You could sit up at one end of the bed, but there was only room for your feet at the other end.

Frid had knocked out a little window in the outer wall, and from it she could see the crest of the hill, with the sea off to the left.

A chair stood beside the bed. There were three pegs on the paneled wall beside the door for her clothes. On the floor lay a brown goatskin rug, and there were curtains at the window. Looking more closely at them, Eidi recognized the light-brown material with the golden leaves that she had once long ago had a dress made of.

The room was not very big, but it was hers, and she thought it was the most beautiful room she had ever seen.

"Thank you," she said to Frid, who was standing in the door. "Thank you very, very much."

"Well, I just thought it was time you had your own room. Come and see what else I made."

Tink and Eidi followed him up the stairs. He had made a real room in the loft for Ravnar, and he promised to build one for Tink in the opposite end gable. Until then, Tink and Ravnar would have to share.

Foula called them. Supper was ready. Cam was awake, and Foula had brought him in from the settle bed and set him in his basket by the hearth.

He no longer looked like a pale little frog but had grown into a real, chubby baby with dimpled cheeks and hair on his head. Eidi brought out the jacket she had knitted for him, and it just fit.

Ravnar came back with Myna and Doup. He

brought them up from the shore, where they had been gathering driftwood.

Myna was wearing her hair up, just like Foula, and Eidi thought it made her look grown up. But the old dark-blue dress was the same, only more worn, and now it was too short at the wrists, and tight over the chest.

"Why Eidi, where's your hair?" she said in her well-remembered, rather hoarse voice.

Eidi hugged her and said, "I cut it off."

Doup had grown into a long-limbed boy, a bit too big for his trousers, but with the same fair hair and the same blue eyes. He was shy with Eidi at first, but when they had eaten he climbed onto her lap and made her sing all his favorite songs.

It was late in the evening before Eidi finished telling the whole story of her travels. Doup was sleeping on Myna's lap, and Tink had fallen asleep in the old settle bed, so they decided not to disturb him but let him sleep there that night. Ravnar saw Myna and Doup home, and Frid carried Cam in his basket into the bedroom.

Foula was about to bank the fire with ashes so that the embers would last the night when Eidi offered to do it later. She wanted to sit in the living room by the fire for a while. So Foula kissed her good night and closed the door after her.

The fire crackled, a mouse rustled in a corner of the room, and it gradually came over Eidi that she was home.

18

"You'll have to tell her."

Frid's voice came through the crack of the half-open door to the main room, together with a strip of light.

Eidi was standing in the dark passage with her hand on the door latch of her new room. She stayed there, stock-still.

"I was so young then," said Foula, "and he was such a charmer. All the girls were after him, and I was so flattered when it was suddenly me he was courting.

"But he told me right at the offset that no matter what happened, he wouldn't marry me. He didn't want to marry anyone. So I never told him I was with child."

Cam whimpered, and she hushed him with little, tender sounds.

"I remember the last time we were together. He wanted to give me a gold brooch that had been his mother's. But I wouldn't take it. Perhaps I should have taken it after all, so that Eidi would have something from her father's family."

Eidi lifted the latch quietly and closed the door after her. Then she threw herself on the bed and put her hands over her ears. But it was too late. She had heard it. And she had understood. Bandon was her father.

The rising sun turned the whitewashed walls rosy. The house was full of sounds: Cam prattling, Foula clattering with the pans in the kitchen, Doup's little laugh, Frid's and Ravnar's voices as they wished each other good morning, Tink's cautious steps coming down the stairs right over her bed.

Then there was a knock at the bedroom door, and Foula stepped in with a mug of piping hot tea. She gave it to Eidi and sat down on the edge of the bed.

"I'm so glad to have you home," she said after a

while. "I almost didn't recognize you. Who's that tall lad with the curly hair? I thought. You've grown taller by half a head."

Eidi laughed.

"I thought you were at Rossan's all this time," Foula went on in a more hesitant and serious tone. "But now that you've met Bandon, I think you ought to know—"

"That he's my father."

Foula looked at her without a word, taken aback. Then she asked, "How did you know?"

"I believe I dreamed it," Eidi answered evasively.

Two deep furrows appeared between her mother's brows. "Did he say anything?"

"No, he doesn't know about it."

"Oh," she said, and the furrows gradually smoothed themselves out. "It doesn't really matter anymore. And you may never see him again, come to that."

She gave Eidi's legs a quick pat and got up. "What do you say to getting dressed? Some little boys are asking for you."

Doup and Tink followed her like two puppies while Eidi made the rounds of Crow Cove.

She showed Tink the cow and the sheep grazing on the steep hillsides, the eagles circling high overhead, and the place where everyone dipped water from the brook.

Then they crossed the brook to visit Myna. She wasn't at home when they came into the main room at the end of the house. But Eidi sat down anyway, together with the two boys, and looked around her.

The room looked just as she remembered and loved it: the honey-yellow, varnished furniture; the settles with the elaborate carved borders of birds and twining flowers along their backs; the wide bed covered with skins; the fireplace where a log was smoldering under a layer of ash.

The shotgun was not hanging in its place over the mantel, so Myna must have gone hunting.

They went back across the bridge and up by the kitchen garden. Foula was busy sowing all the seeds she had saved from last year, as well as the ones Rossan had sent her. Garden sorrel and horseradish from last year had already sprouted, the one with light-green leaves, the other with dark-green billowy ones, just inside the garden gate.

A little farther down toward the shore, Ravnar

and Frid were cultivating a new patch for potatoes, because there was no more room in the old enclosure.

They had picked all the stones out of the ground and made a wall of them around the new patch, to keep the sheep out. Now they were bringing a big load of seaweed on Doup's little brown horse, to enrich the soil.

"Why don't you use Tink's and my mare?" asked Eidi.

"That's for Foula to decide," answered Frid, lifting the baskets of seaweed off the little horse's back. He went up to the opposite end of the field to empty them.

Foula was nursing Cam on the bench in front of the house. He was so big now that when he sat on her knee he could reach her breast.

"Ow," Foula complained. "If you're going to use your teeth, I'll give you something else to chew on."

She pushed his head aside and buttoned up her blouse, though he whimpered. Then she looked up at Eidi.

"Well, is it nice to be home again?"

Eidi smiled and nodded. "It surely is."

"And what about you, Tink? Do you like it here?"

He took hold of Eidi's hand before he nodded, too.

"Why can't they use our mare?" asked Eidi.

"Well, Lesna and Kotka made a really good bargain there. She's in foal, so I don't think we should work her too hard."

"Then we'll have two horses," exclaimed Tink happily, looking up at Eidi. "One each. I'd like to have the little one."

"That you shall," she said, smiling at him. She gave his hand a squeeze before letting it go.

Then she reached out and took Cam up in her arms.

"Yes, you take him awhile, will you?" said Foula, rising and returning to her work in the garden.

"Hello there, you little rascal," said Eidi, rubbing her nose against Cam's round cheek with a soft growl.

He looked startled at first, but when she had done it once or twice more, he squealed with delight and didn't want her to stop.

But she did stop when she noticed that Tink was standing there pulling at her skirts, not wanting to be left out. She sat down on the bench and patted the place beside her.

"Come and sit down, Tinkerlink."

Then she took Cam on one knee and Tink on the other and sang the song for them about the rag rug of life, with the gray warp and the gay weft of colored tatters.

Ravnar came by just as the song ended. He grinned at her.

"You're a queer one," he said. "You leave home because you get one little brother, and then you bring another one back with you."

She laughed, throwing an arm around Tink, and sang so loud that it could be heard all over the cove.

Eidi was alone in the living room. She was darning the holes in the sleeve of Kotka's old, worn sweater. When she had finished, she spread the sweater out on the table before folding it up. As she smoothed out the front, she felt the golden brooch still pinned on the inside. She undid it, took it in her hand, and looked at it.

The arrow was the length of her little finger, pointed at one end and with two small, ridged fans at the other, to represent the feathers. It was bent a little out of shape, but not enough to prevent it from concealing the pin on the back.

She closed her hand on the brooch and went over to the fireplace. The fire had burned down to embers, a glowing red heap against the blackened stones. She sat on her heels and felt the heat on her face. The light from the embers came and went. It was as if the fire was breathing soundlessly.

One single move of her hand, and she would see the arrow melt to golden drops and disappear in gray-white ashes.

She listened for the tone in her ear. But all was still, and she knew that the howling noise had gone forever.

Then she saw that at this moment it was entirely up to her whether to keep the gold pin or not. And no matter what she did, Bandon would always be her father. And no matter who her father was, she would always be Eidi.

She brought her hand up to her breast and fastened the golden arrow on the front of her dress. Then she put more wood on the fire and sat looking into the flames.